CRUSHED

A gripping crime thriller full of twists

EMMY ELLIS

Detective Tracy Collier Book 2

Originally published as *All That Deceit*

JOFFE BOOKS

Revised edition 2024
Joffe Books, London
www.joffebooks.com

First published in Great Britain in 2018
as *All That Deceit*

This paperback edition was first published
in Great Britain in 2024

Cover art by Dee Dee Books Covers

ISBN: 978-1-83526-351-8

PROLOGUE

"You bloody little bastard!"

I say it to him because it's true. He *is* a bastard — plus, he behaves like some annoying brat in an adult body only a mother could love. People say he's a nice fella, do anything for anyone, but they don't know him like I do.

They don't know how much he's ruined my life.

I've often thought about suffocating him. You know, waiting until he's asleep, mouth gaping, and placing a pillow over his face and pushing, pushing, pushing . . .

"Would you *please* stop saying things like that to me?" he asks, brow all squished up, like he's mortally wounded by what I've said.

Needs to grow a pair, that one. And *will* I stop saying things?

No.

"Oh, so I can't voice my *opinion* now?" I stare at him, and my eyes hurt at the back where they're bulging.

He has that effect on me.

"Some opinions shouldn't be aired," he says.

Oh, really now? Since when?

"I'll say what I sodding well like. Always have, always will since . . ." I purse my lips. The cheek of him. Who does he think he is?

"I'm leaving now." He rises. Sighs. The weight of the world on his shoulders, he slouches off towards the front door.

I stay where I am in my comfy chair. He'll be back. Usually is. They say you can't keep kicking a dog, because one day he'll bite you. This one won't. Spineless, that's what he is.

No guts.

The front door shuts with a soft *snick*, and I pull my notebook out from under my seat. It has all my plans in it, little things I've jotted down over the years. A slight sheen of dust covers the matt grey front, probably from where I swept the hardwood floors the other day. That's what dust does, doesn't it? Gets on everything, everywhere.

That's what he is, dust.

Or he soon will be if I have my way.

His urn will be so pretty.

CHAPTER ONE

"I don't believe it. Tracy bloody Collier, hair as red as ever!"

"Kane Barnett. What are the odds, eh?" Tracy smiled and walked up to him in the incident room, relieved to see her old friend grinning. She'd dreaded the kind of reception she'd get from him. Maybe he thought she was just visiting the station . . .

She'd moved here last week, heading up the serious crimes squad, starting today. Stepping on Kane's toes, shoving him aside while she took over. He'd carried the workload up until now — damn good copper, he was — but this place had gone to shit lately, criminals crawling out of the proverbial woodwork. And after her latest case in the place she used to live, she needed a new start. Away from the memories. The horror of a killer orchestrating murders committed by someone else. Away from all those lies.

Her partner and boyfriend, Damon Hanks, stood beside her, remaining quiet like she'd asked him to. Best she deal with this bombshell.

"What are you doing here then?" Kane asked.

Poor bastard hasn't been told.

"Um, I'm here for the meeting with Chief Winter." God, she felt such a bitch. Muscling in on someone else's patch wasn't the greatest way to start a working relationship. Although their ranks were the same, because of the squad she'd be running, he'd have to defer to her.

Hashtag ouch.

"Oh right." His smile tightened a bit.

Twigging, was he? Penny dropping?

"What's been happening in this neck of the woods?" she asked, a subject change better than going into dodgy territory.

"Biggest job was me dealing with some nutter killing people in his street, as well as a sex worker. Unpleasant to say the least." He grimaced as though the case had affected him more than any other.

Probably got emotionally involved.

She understood how the fuck *that* worked.

"Ah, I heard about that. Also kidnapped a teenager, didn't he?" She knew what had happened, she'd read the file, but it didn't hurt to get his take on it, his feelings. He'd undoubtedly changed since she'd last seen him, had become a different type of officer. If she could get his measure, it'd make working with him easier. For both of them.

"I have to say it was the worst case of my career. The things he did . . . Shoved some old dear on a bonfire, blow-torched the teenager, suffocated the sex worker." He shook his head, spots of deep pink colouring his cheeks. "Sickest person I've ever encountered."

No. The sickest person was—

She cleared her throat, her mind. "Sounds nasty. Did you take counselling?"

He shook his head. "Thought about it but . . . No."

Me neither.

She'd promised herself she'd get help to talk everything through but hadn't got around to it. After her sessions with a therapist, Dr Schumer, during that last big case, she had trust issues. Hell, she'd had trust issues before that. She'd never know if the doctor had been in on the whole thing and her talking to him had been a part of the plan.

"Difficult, isn't it," she said, "to talk to people about what you've been through, what you've seen?"

Kane nodded. Shoved his hands through his hair and gripped it. Bad habit or anxiety? "Anyway, enough about that. So, this meeting—"

"Chief Winter would like you all to come through now."

Tracy turned. A female in a power suit — black trousers and jacket, cream blouse, sturdy copper's shoes — stood holding the door open.

"Ah, thanks, Nada," Kane said.

Tracy smiled at her — there was another surprise in store for Kane regarding this woman — and the members of his team rose from their desks, abandoning whatever work they'd been doing. The absence of clicking keyboards, the shuffling of papers, and the low mumble of folks on the phone lent an ominous air to the moment. The calm before the possible shitstorm.

Why did I agree to do this again?

Everyone filed out, Tracy holding back with Damon. They remained in the permanent incident room, and Tracy waited for the door to close.

"All right, Trace?" Damon asked.

"This might have been a bad move on Winter's part," she said. "Kane hasn't got a clue."

"Not your problem. You're here to do a job. *We're* here to do one. We had to get away, and this was the perfect opportunity. We can start afresh here. The proper Tracy can come out." He winked. "She's been peeking through the old ones these last few weeks, and I like her."

He referred to her multiple sides, where she'd taken on different personas over the years to get her through certain situations. Some would say she was a fuck-up — she'd say it herself — but Damon said she just needed a little fixing. Better than a complete overhaul, though, so she'd take it.

"Pretend you don't have a history with Kane," Damon said. "A quick shag or two when you were younger doesn't count."

Tracy inwardly cringed. Although she was grateful Damon wasn't the jealous type and could bring things up without being bothered by it, the reminder of her few nights with Kane wasn't something she wanted to dwell on.

"Christ," she said. "Shh, will you?"

"Just letting you know how I feel about it. You're with me now, so . . ."

"We need to get to that meeting. Bad impression straight off the bloody bat, isn't it, leaving them waiting."

She pushed the door open and fast-paced it down the corridor to the meeting room. Inside, she headed for the empty seat beside Winter, as she'd been advised to do earlier that morning, and Damon sat to her left. Kane was at the other end, directly opposite her, and his flushed cheeks and stony glare indicated he had some idea of what Tracy was doing there, considering she now occupied Kane's usual seat — another titbit from Winter.

"Right," Winter said, the word coming out as a gust, the scent of coffee wafting off it. "Straight to the point, as per usual . . ." He scrubbed his grey-speckled stubble, fingertips massaging. "We've come to the conclusion we need a serious crimes squad based here that will encompass the whole county. DI Tracy Collier will be in charge—"he indicated her with an open hand — "partnered by Damon Banks." Again, he gestured. "Kane, you'll also be on the team, along with Nada. Lara and Tim, same goes for you."

Silence.

"I realise this might be a surprise," Winter went on, "but I'm sure you'll all settle into your new roles admirably. With two sets of partners in the team, this should ease the stress for Tracy and Damon — likewise Kane and Nada."

He continued with an update on all ongoing cases, and Tracy zoned out, having read the files over the past week prior to her arrival. There wasn't much going on right now — the investigation on a drug dealer, Jez Pickins, had been closed owing to his death, and the man Kane had been searching for with regards to the bonfire/sex worker/teenage kidnap case was now in HM Prison Dartmoor for a long stretch. The usual cases of fraud and whatnot weren't taking up much of the team's time, so Tracy had to wonder what the hell she'd be doing. Twiddling her thumbs until someone committed murder most probably.

Don't tempt fate.

"So," Winter said, "let's get to it. Tracy is aware of all cases and has a plan going forward. Kane, you'll need to get together and work out your roles. No sulking." He chuckled. "It's not a demotion, just a new way of doing things. Thank you. On you go."

Everyone rose at the same time, the screech of chairs on the lino a bit harsh on the old ears. Tracy winced at that and the filthy look Kane directed at her. She'd pegged him as someone who'd just get on with things, but it seemed he had issues.

Great. She needed that like a case of haemorrhoids. Shame she couldn't sort Kane out with a suppository.

She left the room to enter her new office, a cubby hole really, but was glad she hadn't been ordered to take Kane's. That would really be rubbing TCP on the ulcer. Damon would work in the incident room with the others, as would Nada, and those from Kane's original team, bar Lara and Tim, would be on hand for big investigations but used elsewhere on other squads the rest of the time. Erica seemed put out, but Alastair appeared the easy-going type who wasn't that bothered.

Tracy had reason to be hated, but that was all right. She was used to it.

She unpacked a few things to take her mind off the meeting she'd be having with her new team. She doubted it would be pretty, but they'd get over it. Eventually. And if they didn't?

Tough.

About to place her pens in the top drawer of her desk, Tracy glanced up in shock at Kane barging into the room.

Oh. It's like that, is it?

"Ever heard of knocking?" she asked, raising her eyebrows. She didn't deal well with egos.

"You could have warned me," he said, hands on hips, a kid angry at not being captain of the footy team anymore.

Grow the eff up.

"I could," she said, "had I been allowed." She mirrored his stance, more to take the piss than anything. "If this is going to be a problem, feel free to put in for a transfer. I'm not in the habit of pandering to hurt feelings or low self-esteem — I'm here to do a job. The fact it makes me your superior, despite the matching rank, isn't my fault. Got a beef about it, go and see Winter."

She strode to her door and stood there with her arm out.

On your bike, mate.

"So that's it? No discussion?" he asked, a fuck-off big frown adding to his belligerent child expression.

"We've had the discussion. There isn't anything else to say." She smiled. "Except maybe: You remember how it was before you headed a team, when you ran things by your superior?"

He grimaced.

"Remember it again," she said. "It's a prerequisite for your new role." She hadn't wanted to be a cow, but he'd asked for it by not knocking before entering. He'd learn she hadn't changed that much since they'd last been together. Still hard-nosed. Still didn't suffer fools gladly. "It won't take long to get used to it."

He stalked out, almost knocking her with his shoulder. She'd have hauled him over the coals for it if he had. Seemed she had a tosser on her hands. She'd bet he'd make things difficult and all.

Fabulous.

She followed him, and he swanned into his office down the corridor. To brood. To curse her to Hell and back.

Oh, jog on.

Tracy entered the main room, cringing at Erica and Alastair gathering their things, emptying desks. "Guys, hold it for a second, please."

They turned to look at her.

"Before you go off to your new posts, I'd like you in on this meeting because I've no doubt you'll be back here to help out periodically, and it'll save me the job of repeating myself later. Nada, please could you ask Kane to join us? Thank you."

Nada smiled, seemingly cheerful about the recent turn of events, and Tracy had a feeling she'd grow to like the woman, given time. Tracy wasn't a fan of making friends, especially as the relationship with her current, only mate was strained more than reused tea leaves. She was supposed to sort out their differences before she'd left but couldn't face the hassle. Kathy, the pathologist in Tracy's old area, had got a hornet up her arse about Tracy not spending much time with her lately. Bonus at getting away and beginning a new life? No Kathy to contend with.

She'd do well with Kane. Stroppy pair of buggers.

She hid a smile and glanced at Damon, who, bless him, knew how to behave at work. He might not like some of her decisions, but he didn't act out. Much.

Breaking the awkward silence with an exaggerated sigh, Kane returned with Nada. Kane sat on the edge of a desk belonging to Lara, crossing his ankles, folding his arms over his chest.

Body language spoke a million words.

"Right then." Tracy swept her gaze over everyone then focused on the empty whiteboard at the far end beside two others with minimal writing and images on them. "From now on, anything you'd usually ask Kane, you ask me. Any orders regarding cases will come from me. If you don't do this and continue to approach Kane, or take orders from Kane without my permission, I won't be aware of everything going on, which, to be blunt — and you'll soon realise how blunt I can be — can royally fuck up an investigation. It's *imperative* you stick to these rules. Anyone found not doing so will be reported to Chief Winter." She gave a tight smile. "No, I don't take any shit if anyone was wondering. I don't cover for anyone, I don't give any leeway. You're paid to do this job, and you'll do it by my rules. If you're feeling this isn't the team for you, again, speak to Winter."

No one appeared to want to say anything.

Okay, she'd push them.

"Anyone have anything they'd like to ask?"

"Does the not covering and leeway apply to your boyfriend, too?" Kane.

What an arsehole.

"Yes, it applies to everyone." Tracy pointed at her partner. "Damon Hanks here is my right-hand man — at work *and* in my private life — but that *does not* mean he gets cut any slack. He'll be the first to tell you that. At work, it's just that — work. If anything, I'm harsher on him because of our personal attachment. Anything else?"

"If I have a lead," Kane said, "I'm taking it I also have to run it by your first."

"Hmm." She tapped her foot. "Seems my little speech just now wasn't clear enough. *No one* is to do anything without running it by me — including you, Kane. I realise you ran your own team, but this is a *new* one, and *I* run this one. Like I said, any issues, see Winter."

Her false smile was going to break her damn face if she wasn't careful.

Her fist was going to break Kane's nose if *he* wasn't careful.

"I will do," Kane said.

"Maybe you need a few days off, Kane," Tracy suggested. "You know, to come to terms with everything. I appreciate this has come as a bit of a shock, but I'm not here to massage any bruised egos. I'm here to catch criminals."

"Something's criminal all right," Kane muttered.

"And what would that be?" Tracy asked. "Me heading the team instead of you? Might as well just get it out into the open, eh? Say what you've got to say."

He tightened his arms about his torso. Flushed a little. Stuck his bottom lip out.

"Nothing to say?" she asked. "I mean, the floor is all yours, may as well take it while you can." She widened her eyes. "Better out than in, so they say. Keeping it in can be detrimental to what we want to achieve. It can ruin the running of a team. Or is that your intention?"

His flush deepened.

Got you nailed, fucker.

"Right, so if that's all on *that* matter, we'll move on to the current cases . . ."

Kane dipped his head, staring at the carpet, and Tracy imagined he was silently calling her all the names he could think of. Bitch would do. That covered everything.

"Now, there will be times where two women will be needed to speak to the families of victims, or victims of rape for example, when a female approach would be better for the person in question. At those times, I'll be partnered with Nada and—"

"So you're poaching my partner now *as well?*" Kane asked, head snapping up. He stared at her as though his whole life was on the verge of collapse.

"I'm not poaching anyone. I'm using the staff available to me for the best results." Tracy glared at him. "Kane, it's clear you aren't happy with this new arrangement. If your game is to throw spanners in the works at every opportunity, *I'll* be going to see Winter. Do you understand what I'm saying?"

"You always were an uncompromising bi—"

"Okay. I see it's time for full disclosure, team. Let's lay it all out so everyone can understand why Kane might be somewhat prickly." *Prick is right.* "I had a sexual relationship with Kane years ago. He's clearly got an issue with me, so please ignore his childish outbursts while he gets his angst out of his system. Some people can't separate business and pleasure and need a little time to adjust. While Kane's doing that, it's best we ignore any untoward remarks that might pop out of his mouth in the adaption process. After all, we're here to work, to help people, to catch criminals, *not* return to high school behaviour, which will inevitably get in the way of our jobs. If everyone else is up for doing your best instead of being an arsewipe, that's grand."

He'd been about to call her a bitch, so her name-calling attack on him was justified.

Or so she told herself anyway.

CHAPTER TWO

Notes:
Next time, remember the element of surprise is to my advantage.

It's done. It didn't quite go to plan, so it just goes to show no matter how much you prepare, reality isn't as you expect. For one, he was stronger than I imagined — bloody hell was he strong — and I picked up a knock to the cheek. I'm hoping it doesn't bruise, as I have a lunch date with Beryl tomorrow, and having her asking a million and one questions will just get on my last nerve. I like Beryl, I do, but she's a bit like *him*. Can't take the truth. Asks me not to say certain things like he does, too.

If you can't stand the heat, get out of the kitchen.

His murder turned out a bit sloppy. I shouldn't beat myself up, though, it was my first time in a long while. This method will get better as I go along, I'm sure. I've been building up to this point for years, and now I'm here, it seems everything is slotting into place.

I'm finally going to get a measure of peace.

Darkness helps. I must write that in my notes. I didn't feel exposed at all; didn't sense anyone's attention on me at any time. Except his. The subject, I mean. Who would take any notice of me anyway? It's not like I stand out, is it? I'm just your average Joe, as they say. When people think of murderers, they imagine glaring eyes with a manic glint, don't they, someone holding up a knife or a gun. In my case, it was something else entirely.

Oh, for Pete's sake. Sounds like *he's* here for another visit. Got his finger pressed to the bell button as though it needs constant ringing because I'm deaf. I thought he wouldn't be back for a while, seeing as he'd stropped off last time. He usually leaves me be for a while if I'm what he calls *acerbic*.

I push myself out of my chair and head to the front door. He's there — the shape of him through the gauzy glass panel churns my stomach — and I've got the urge to do him in already. But no. I need to wait.

I swing the door open, and he smiles his absurd grin, the one that has me wanting to punch his teeth in. Refraining from doing that, I step back so he can enter. He lumbers in, out of breath from his asthma — and wasn't that a pest in the past? Like I enjoyed sitting in Accident and Emergency while he wheezed away, clutching at his throat.

Lord, give me strength.

"What do you want?" I shut the door.

"Charming, that is." He takes off his scarf and coat, hangs them on the hooks he put up for me. They're wonky; he's useless. "Do you treat all your guests this way?" He sounds like he's getting a cold, all nasal and bunged up.

He'd better not pass it on to me.

"Didn't you get your flu jab like I reminded you?" God, do I have to do everything?

"I did, but I'm still able to catch colds, you know."

He says it like I'm thick.

Ignoring him, I bustle off into the kitchen — making tea will give me something to do with my hands other than harming him.

"Not out for lunch with Beryl today?" he asks, trotting in and plunking himself down at the little table in the corner. The chair creaks with his weight.

Wouldn't surprise me if the leg snapped off.

I sigh. "No, lunch with Beryl is on *Tues*days." How many times do I have to tell him that? "And if I *was* out to lunch with her today, I wouldn't be standing here, would I?"

"All right, keep your hair on." He sniffs.

"I'll keep my hair on the day you stop acting dumb. Always were dumb, you, and I'm fair sick of it." I slosh boiled water into the teapot, and some of it splashes onto the worktop. *For fu* . . . "Aren't you meant to be at work? What is it, a case of lazy-itis? Got a dribbling nose so you can't go in? I don't know, people today . . . They've only got to have a headache and they're off sick for a week. No staying power."

"I'm not allowed to go in with a cold. I could pass it on to the patients," he says, his tone that of someone weary.

"Well, they're on their last legs anyway, so what does it matter?" I plonk the teapot on the table and pop a knitted cosy over the top. Two cups follow, one on each of the coasters, along with the milk jug and sugar pot.

"That's a horrible thing to say." He *tsks*.

"What's horrible, the truth? These people are having treatments for the *disease*, aren't they. Once they're in the hospital for that, there's no turning back. You've said it yourself, so your sniffles are hardly likely to change the buggering outcome, are they?"

I sit opposite him then wish I hadn't. Means I have to *see* him, even if it's only out of the corner of my eye. I've had enough of the sight of him to last me a lifetime. I move to stand by the sink.

"What's the matter, do I smell?" He laughs at his ridiculous joke.

"Don't you always? Deodorant is a thing, you know."

He shakes his head, and I want to be strong enough to grip hold of it, twist it off his wide neck, and throw it at the wall.

He fills his cup with tea. "You just can't help yourself, can you." He adds milk and two sugars. One would be enough, but he's always been a greedy shit.

"Can't help myself with what?" Well, if he's not pouring me any tea, I'll have to do it myself, won't I.

"Being spiteful," he clarifies, as if I didn't know what he meant. "That acerbic tongue of yours will get you into trouble one day. Not everyone is as mild-mannered as me. Someone will take a pop at you at some point, you mark my words."

If he says *acerbic* one more time . . .

I don't deign to answer and busy myself with my drink.

"We're moving away," he says, out of the damn blue.

What?

Ordinarily, I'd find this news amazing, but not now. Not when I've set my plan in motion. He always, *always* has to mess things up. Every. Bloody. Time. Not seeing him, his scutty wife, and their whiny, entitled little bastard kids would have made my day in the past, but now he's ruined it. That's going to set me up for a bad lunch date with Beryl, isn't it. I won't be able to get into a good mood for days because of this.

"Where are you going?" Not that I care.

"Scotland."

Scotland? Dear God, does he know about . . . ? "When?" My heart skips a beat.

"Oh, not for a few months yet. My new position up there won't be available for a while."

Thank you, Lord.

"I see. And what about Sarah?" His imbecile wife. "Is she remaining a stay-at-home mother? You know, still relying on you to provide when there's adequate day care out there and she could put in a bit of hard graft herself?" I don't think about the fact I stayed home to bring *him* up.

"You know we prefer her at home while the children are still small. Once they go to school full time, she—"

He sounds like . . . someone I don't want to think about.

"A likely story if ever I heard one." I snort. He hates that. "She'll come up with some excuse not to work, that one."

"I'll not have you bad-mouthing my wife. You can say whatever you like to me, but don't put Sarah down."

"Why not? She's an extension of you by marriage. I can say what I like."

He stands and walks to the kitchen doorway without even drinking any of his tea. That's a waste, that is.

"You know, I came back today hoping the last time I was here you were just in a bad mood, but you're *always* in a bad mood." He sighs. "Nothing is ever good enough for you. Everything has a black side instead of a bright one. I'm surprised Beryl can stand you. I'm off, and I don't think I'll be back this time."

"Sod off, then. The sooner you do, the quicker I'll get peace." *Isn't that the damn truth.*

He disappears into the hallway, and I hug myself, my mood getting better by the second. And him saying he won't be back . . . a load of old codswallop.

The front door clicks shut — he hasn't even got the bottle to slam it — and I smile, satisfied at having pissed him off. It's so easy to do. He has far too many hot buttons.

I throw his tea down the sink then open a window to air the place out — his germs and the result of the lack of anti-perspirant don't belong in my home. Tea in hand, I return to my comfy chair to make new notes.

* * *

The Past

Alfie — "Call me Alfie, love. Sir is far too stuffy!" — has asked me out on a date.

I can hardly believe it. For a start, I thought he was more interested in Beryl or one of the others, not some dowdy little thing like me.

Beryl is my best friend. I hope she isn't upset if I take Alfie up on his offer. She's fancied him ever since we started working here.

Is it okay to go out with your boss? I'm not sure, especially because he's older than me. Can I even cancel? Will that mean I'll lose my job?

It's too late. He's here. Waiting at the bottom of the front garden. I told him not to come to the door. I don't want Mum and Dad embarrassing me. They'll want him to come in so they can see if he's got the Trustworthy Look *as Dad puts it. Of course Alfie's trustworthy. He's an accountant.*

I rush outside and fly down the path, out of breath by the time I reach him. He smiles, and my stomach flips. Is this it? Is this what love feels like?

We catch a matinee at the cinema, and Alfie holds my hand every so often, and I hold my breath, wondering if he'll kiss me, but he doesn't. There's still time for that, and we leave the picture house and go to the café next door. Alfie orders for us, and he's a gentleman and pays the bill. We sit and eat our sandwiches, and a dollop of pickle squeezes out of mine and latches on to my face beside my mouth. Heat rushes to my cheeks — I've never been so embarrassed in my life — but thankfully Alfie doesn't see it. He's staring at something over my shoulder.

While he's occupied, I wipe the mess off and eat the rest quickly so by the time he looks at me again, my food will be gone. But there he is, still staring at whatever, and I can't resist turning around to see what has him rudely ignoring me.

A lady sits there, a baby cradled in her arm, and a young child, about three years old, is beside her munching on a sticky bun.

I clear my throat. "Do you know her?"

Alfie blinks, as though he's been in the biggest trance, and shifts his gaze to me. "Oh . . . No. I was just . . . I'd love to have children, wouldn't you?"

Of course I would, it's my dream to be married one day and have several beautiful babies. Isn't that what every woman wants? "Yes. You have to be married first, though."

I don't know why I said that. I'm such a novice with the opposite sex.

"Shall we?" he asks.

"Pardon me?" I blink. What is he saying?

"Shall we get married?"

This is so unexpected. We only know each other through work. All right, that's been around three or four years now, but still . . .

"Me and you?" I bleat.

"Why not?" he says. "You're of good stock—"

"Good stock?" Am I a sheep or cow? A horse?

"Oh, you know what I mean. You're lovely, and we'd be good together, don't you think?"

"What I think is we should date for a while longer before deciding. Every girl wants to be courted. We need to know if we're right for each other."

"You're correct. Of course you are. Shall we set a date for six months then?"

My head spins. Alfie wants us to marry, to have children. I had no idea he had such strong feelings for me.

I think I'm about to faint.

CHAPTER THREE

Back in her office with Damon, Tracy sipped some vending machine coffee, mindful not to burn her tongue like she always did. She stared at Damon from behind her desk, him sitting on the chair opposite.

"Christ, what a penis," he said.

"Hmm. He wasn't always like this. Something's obviously eating at him."

"Um, yeah, you."

"No." She shook her head, the movement damn near sloshing coffee over her hand. "More than me. More than this situation."

"Whatever it is, he needs to leave it behind when he walks through the door to work. Look at how you ran the last team with everything you had going on."

He had a point. She'd managed to get on with things despite the Past, despite being a victim of child abuse. And she intended to carry on the same way. Although her abusers were dead, she still had some things gnawing at her conscience. Like killing one of them. She hadn't told Damon and didn't think she ever would. He was a by-the-book copper for the most part, and knowing she'd murdered a bloke, had faked it to look like someone else had done it, well, it wasn't his style to keep that quiet no matter how much he loved her.

And she wouldn't expect him to.

"Yes," she said. "It's best to keep on trucking. Move on to the next big case — which is fuck all right now. Suppose we'd better help solve the current ones while we wait for something new. It's not like criminals go on hiatus for that long, is it? Something's bound to turn up."

A knock at the door had her lifting her eyebrows.

"Ask and you shall receive?" she said.

"Maybe." Damon sipped his coffee.

"Come in," she called.

Nada opened the door halfway and poked her head round it. "Um, ma'am, Kane's had news of a murder, and he's um . . . he's briefing everyone."

"Is he now." Tracy smiled at her and placed her coffee on the desk, itching to wrap her hands around Kane's throat and strangle the fucker. "Thanks for informing me. Where does he think you are?"

"Toilet, ma'am."

"I'll give you three minutes. Oh, and if you have to call me something, it's 'boss', all right?"

"Okay, boss." Nada winked and closed the door.

"She'll go far, that one," Tracy said.

"You're calm, considering. Taken a chill pill, have you?" Damon smirked.

"Oh, believe me, I'm well dogged off."

"I'm looking forward to the fireworks. Shame we don't have popcorn to hand."

"Shut your face." She grinned. "You know, he's seriously going to get on my tits if he keeps on."

"He'd better bloody not."

"Full of the quips today, aren't you." She glanced at the wall clock then picked up the phone and pressed speed dial for the front desk.

"Vic Atkins," the sergeant said.

"Hi, DI Tracy Collier here. I'm going to give you the benefit of the doubt on this one, as you might not be aware of what's going on, but I'm heading the new serious crimes squad, so anything that comes in, you speak to me, *not* DI Barnett, all right?"

"Oh. Right. Hello, ma'am. It's just that Kane said—"

"Doesn't matter what Kane said. Everything comes to me — no matter if he tells you different. I don't want him putting you in any awkward positions either, so if you're unsure — say he asks you to do something for him that I would normally do as team leader — just let me know. I'll be down shortly to introduce myself and give you my mobile numbers — work and private. That way, you can always contact me."

That way you have no excuse.

"Okay, ma'am. Sorry. Didn't realise what was going on. Kane gave me the impression things should stay as they were before."

"Well, Kane is finding it a little difficult to adjust, so . . . What job has come in? The one you told Kane about?"

"A murder, ma'am. Man found in the local park beside the stream there. Gilbert has been informed."

"Gilbert's the pathologist, yes?"

"Yes, ma'am."

"Boss is better."

"Uh, right. Erm . . . boss."

"Address, please. I'm new to the area, so bear with me."

He rattled it off. "Is that all, boss?"

"For now. I'll see you in a bit." She returned the phone to its cradle. "That sneaky little shit . . ."

Damon shook his head. "I can imagine."

"Come on," she said and left the office.

In the incident room, Kane stood by the whiteboards, the empty one now decorated with his scrawl. He gave directions as though her earlier ones were of no consequence and didn't even flinch at the sight of her. Tamping down anger, she strode to stand beside him.

"Right, straight away, my authority has been ignored," she said. "Sit down, please, Kane."

He didn't.

"Really?" she said. "You're really going to do this?"

He clamped his lips together.

"Okay, guys, here's the deal." She tucked her arms behind her back. "All but two of you clearly don't care about the welfare of the squad and how it's run. Damon does, and someone else does — that someone informed me that Kane was continuing as team leader, addressing you all. If you'd just give me five minutes, I have a chief to see. Perhaps then you'll do as you're told. Do not — I repeat *do not* — act on anything DI Barnett has told you. Thank you. Kane, I'm asking you in front of witnesses not to go to the crime scene. Damon and I will deal with that. As you were."

She walked out, heart thumping. She understood how they must be feeling, but the one piece of advice she'd given to her old team before she'd left — and fuck, she wished they were here now — was to start with a clean slate and accept the ways of their new DI and not harp on about how she used to run things.

Outside Winter's door, she took a deep breath then knocked.

"Enter."

She went in, closed the door, and pressed her back against it.

"Ah. Trouble in paradise already?" Winter asked. "Sit. Have a coffee. It works wonders on the old temper." He moved to a coffee machine sitting on a filing cabinet. The sodding thing looked decrepit. "Go on, take a seat."

She obeyed. "Thanks, sir."

"What's he done?" He poured out two cups. "Sugar? Milk?"

"One sugar, and yes, milk, please. Oh, he's only gone and ignored me. I told the team everything had to go by me, not him, and the poor bloke on the desk — Vic, is it? — didn't know of the change, so he told Kane about a new case. Nada came in to inform me Kane was briefing everyone, while I'm in my office none the wiser."

Winter handed her a cup then sat behind his desk. "Hmm. Funny how he's behaving in a way he'd normally despise coming from someone else."

She sipped. "This is nice, thanks."

"Yes, love my coffee machine. Okay . . . His last big case kind of did a number on him. His partner at the time, Richard Lemon, was acting strangely — died, by the way — leaving Kane to carry the can until Kane requested Nada Caridà as his partner. Now, Nada is someone worth getting along with. She's a superb officer and does as she's told. Did you let him know Nada would be working alongside you at times?"

"I did. He accused me of poaching her."

Winter frowned. "That's a strange response. I heard — and don't quote me on this — that during that case I mentioned, Kane was involved with the girlfriend of Jez Pickins. You know, the drug dealer. She's apparently moved away to start again — bit like you, really — so maybe he's upset about that and it's affecting his performance."

"But that case was closed ages ago, sir. The killer was sentenced recently, I'll give you that, but . . ."

"The woman only moved after the trial. Perhaps she broke off their relationship."

"Was he shitty — pardon my French, sir — before I came on the scene as well, then?"

Winter rested his head back on his chair and cradled his cup. "Not that I've seen, no."

"Then his behaviour today is because of me and the new situation. I'm letting you know now that I don't do well with people who don't work from the same rule book as me. Damon, Nada, fine. The others? Kane — I'd gladly see him shipped off if he doesn't pull his socks up, and Lara and Tim . . . they didn't say a word about what Kane was doing."

"Maybe it was awkward for them. If they got up to inform you, he'd know. Which brings up the question: How did Nada do it?"

"She told him she was going to the loo."

"See? Great copper. Thinks on her feet. Right, how has it been left?"

"I've asked the team not to act on anything Kane has told them, and Kane isn't to go to the crime scene. I'm expecting him to go anyway." She drank some more coffee. Winter was right. It did wonders for the temper.

"Okay, let's see what he does when you go back into the incident room. If he's not there . . ."

"Sir, not being funny, but I'm not poncing around with him. I have a body to visit, family members to inform. I don't want to have this case fucked up by him. If he's at the scene, I'll let you know, but right now I need to get to work." She finished her drink then placed the cup on the desk.

"I like your attitude, Tracy. As you told me in your interview, the victims and their families come first. I also like — *liked* — Kane's attitude before today. He was much the same as you — dedicated — so why he's doing this now is a mystery."

"Mystery or not, it's sodding bugging, and he needs to stop it." She stood. "Thanks for hearing me out, sir, but if he's going to continue in this way, I'll ship out to pastures new and let the baby have his toys back. I have no tethers, and Damon will go with whatever I want. No skin off my nose to be going elsewhere."

"No," he said, rising and walking to the door. "You're the best one to head this team. You're staying."

Having heard what she wanted, she said goodbye and returned to the incident room.

As suspected, Kane wasn't there. Nada was.

"Off to the scene, is he?" Tracy asked.

"Yes, boss," Nada said.

"Fine." Tracy forced a smile. "I've had a word with the chief." She stared at Lara and Tim. "If you continue to go against my wishes, the door is open, and my boot print will be on your arse as you exit. If you'd prefer to stay in your current employment, follow my rules. It really is that simple — listening to Kane won't do you any favours. Now, I'm off to the crime scene, and when I get back, *I'll* brief you. For now, please continue with the old cases. Thank you." She jerked her head towards the door. "Damon, come on, please."

She led the way down three flights of stairs then out into the staff parking area. In her car, she started the engine, and while Damon got in, she plugged the details into the satnav.

"Shit. I forgot to say hello to the desk sergeant." She got out. "Won't be a second."

Once she'd given Vic her card and reiterated what she'd told him earlier, she returned to the vehicle. Inside, she paused to catch her breath.

"Five minutes away it says here." She pointed to the satnav. "Let's go and see what's waiting for us. And meet this Gilbert. Hopefully he won't be as caustic as Kathy."

She drove off, the woman's satnav voice giving directions.

"Did you blimmin' change that?" she asked, trying not to laugh.

"Change what?" Damon cleared his throat. "It's always had an Australian accent, you've just been too distracted to notice."

"Bollocks." She laughed, the tension of the morning seeping away somewhat. "Quite nice round here, don't you think? If a little grimy in some areas."

"It'll do for now," he said. "Doesn't matter where we live so long as we're there together."

She smiled at that and, opening her mouth to reply, she was cut short by the instructions to turn left after two hundred yards. Doing as she was told, she stared ahead at the park entrance — two brick pillars with open wrought-iron black gates topped with gold fleur-de-lis.

"This is a bit grand, isn't it?" She drove through into the car park, where several vehicles sat side by side, including two police cars.

Out on the tarmac, she viewed the area. A large expanse of lawn dotted with square flowerbeds to the left. Another patch of grass surrounded by low hedges, benches at the edges and a fountain in the centre. A children's play section to the right, shrieks and laughter bellowing out from kids having a good time.

So where was this bloody stream?

She spotted a map on a sign beside the public toilets on the other side of the car park and made her way there, blipping her car locked with her key fob once Damon got out. He joined her, and she stared at the length of the stream.

"Really? I mean, we could be walking for ages." She sighed and rang the station. "Vic, yes? Okay, good. It's Tracy Collier. Hi. We're at the park. Did you get any information where at the stream we need to be?"

"Yes, ma'am. Boss. Um, if you're in the car park . . . At the end of that big grassy bit, there are hedges and trees. See them?"

She glanced that way. "Yes."

"There's a break in the hedges, right?"

"Yes." Ah. Was that a police cordon going across the gap?

"Through there, and the body's apparently a few metres along."

"Right. Thank you. Any news for me?"

"No, boss. Not seen or spoken to Kane either."

"Good. Thanks. I'll catch you soon."

She ended the call and slipped her phone in her trouser pocket. She set off, Damon keeping up beside her.

"No messing about at this scene," he warned her.

She smiled. Memories came to mind of her breaking protocol and examining bodies before Kathy had. "I can't. That Gilbert fella will be there. We're not first on the scene because . . . Kane. Prat." Anger surged up, and she batted it away. "If he's here, I'm totally ignoring him."

"Can't see you doing that if he baits you."

"I'll be the bigger person here, you'll see."

He coughed, but it sounded like *bullshit*.

"Whatever, Damon. I can control myself when I have to, you know."

They reached the hedge, and a uniformed officer stood on the other side of the tape. He stepped forward, raising his hand.

"DI Tracy Collier," she said. "And this is DS Damon Banks. This is my crime scene." She held up her warrant card.

The officer peered at it. "DI Barnett has already claimed the scene. I—"

"DI Barnett doesn't have that authority anymore unless I say so. I didn't say so." She smiled, lips together. Showing teeth might have him thinking she was nice. "Scene log, please. We need to sign it." She tapped her foot.

"I'll just speak to DI Barnett and—"

"What you'll do is let us through. It doesn't matter whether there are two detective inspectors at the scene, *okay*?"

"But I don't know you . . ."

She conceded that point. "No, you don't. This is our first day here. Please call Vic—"she searched her brain files for the right answer — "Atkins or whatever his name is. Desk sergeant. Ring him. Ask who I am. I'll wait." She smiled again, fuming inside. If she didn't know better, she'd say Kane had warned him she'd arrive and had given some cock and bull story about why she wasn't allowed through.

The officer walked off to use his phone. He came back and grinned. Sheepish wasn't the word. "Sorry, ma'am, it's just . . ."

"It's just nothing." She ducked under the tape. "Like I said, scene log, please."

He produced it, and she signed then passed it to Damon.

"In future . . . What's your name?" she asked.

"PC Newson, ma'am."

"PC Newson, in future, if you're ever at a serious crime scene, it'll be mine, *not* Barnett's. He might accompany me, but . . ." What was the point in explaining? "Thanks for being so careful."

Newson nodded. "Down that way, ma'am." He pointed to her right. "Not far along. Once you reach the bend, you'll see the tent."

She nodded and walked off, steps brisk. The quicker she reached the scene, the quicker she could turf Kane off it — if she decided to go down that road.

Round the bend, yes, there was the tent. Her stomach churned in anticipation — for what she was about to see and also any confrontation with Kane. Although she'd told Damon she'd keep a level head . . .

Promises are made to be broken.

She chuckled despite the grimness of the situation. Damon was usually always right about her actions and reactions.

"Something funny?" he asked, coming up beside her.

"Just you and your predictions."

"You're going to have a mare at him, aren't you . . ."

"Might do. Depends on how he treats me."

A couple of metres in front of the tent, another PC stopped her. Even though she was glad they were doing their jobs, it pissed her off keep being stopped.

"DI Tracy Collier, DS Damon Hanks." She showed her ID.

"Ah, right. Yes, DI Barnett said you might turn up."

She bristled. "Considering it's my scene, then yes, I've turned up." Gritting her teeth, she brushed past him and went to the box containing the forensic suits.

While they put them on, she thought of ways to get back at Kane then decided she might just surprise herself and Damon by taking the high road. What if Kane was doing this to get a rise out of her, to make her leave?

Not fucking likely.

And with that in mind, she stepped inside.

CHAPTER FOUR

He'd been smacked over the head, that much was glaringly obvious. His skull had cracked open, and blood, small grey matter particles, and tiny bone fragments blared the fact that this fella wasn't waking up anytime soon.

Tracy swallowed bile, her stomach muscles tensing. And Damon? As usual, he was off out of the way, heaving behind his hand. He didn't do crime scenes too well, but the more he attended them, the better he'd handle it. Kane stood in the far corner, talking with a SOCO, giving Tracy evil glances every so often. She ignored the pathetic bastard and concentrated on her reason for being there — the victim.

"So, you'd be Tracy then," an older gentleman said.

As he was crouched beside the body, a leather doctor's bag open next to him, she assumed he was the pathologist.

"I am. Gilbert, isn't it?"

"The one and only." He flashed some teeth. "How are you settling in? I'm hoping you'll be more fun than that curmudgeon over there. He doesn't get my dark jokes. Says I shouldn't make quips at a dead person's expense. Maybe not, it isn't the done thing really, is it, but I do it anyway." He grinned wider. "Gets you through. If I didn't laugh, I'd cry, and that wouldn't do us any good."

She smiled, liking him already. "No. Got to have some light relief somewhere, eh? It all gets too much otherwise."

"Exactly. My kind of girl, you are." He winked.

And that wink brought back memories of her old therapist. A chill rippled down her spine. He'd winked at her twice, and she'd hated the mind games he'd played by doing it, him openly admitting he enjoyed screwing with people's heads. For someone in a profession where he was meant to fix people, she'd never understood his reasoning regarding his enjoyment of winding people up.

"Okay," Gilbert said. "This fellow has ID on him. An iPhone. Once Kane gave me the lowdown on the new 'situation', ahem, I didn't give him any details." He rolled his eyes. "He wasn't pleased, but I know the rules. He's a friend and all, but work is work."

"Thank you for your consideration. Not everyone has been . . . that kind."

"There's a time and a place to misbehave, me thinks, and during an investigation isn't one of them. Anyway, back to the main topic, yes?"

Tracy nodded.

"His wallet contained fifty-five quid, two credit cards, and a debit. This wasn't a mugging for money or his phone," he said.

"What are your initial thoughts on the method of murder?" she asked.

"The obvious is a good whack or five to the head. Front of the cranium's cracked, as you can see, some of his brain on show there. Reminds me a bit of that scene from one of the Hannibal films. You know the one?"

She nodded. Swallowed again.

He gave the thumbs up. "Bloody good books, they were, too. Anyway, I don't think that killed this chap, though, oddly enough. Petechiae on the cheeks and below the eyes, across the nose. Thumb prints on the neck. Swollen tongue. Bloodshot eyes."

"Strangulation?" she asked.

"Yes, but I doubt it would have taken the usual four to five minutes to achieve death — he was probably halfway there with the head wounds, poor sod. Therefore, the amount of force and strength needed for choking would also have been reduced — the victim likely didn't struggle; too fatigued by blood loss and his injuries. Or perhaps he *was* strangled first, and when that didn't work, he was battered to death. I do believe it's my first assumption, though. Nothing beneath his fingernails as far as I can tell, see — no defensive skin scrapings. Either way you come at it, this unfortunate bugger isn't pretty anymore, is he? Won't be winning any beauty contests."

Tracy bit her lip to stop a smile. Gilbert's humour was revolting, but it eased the tension. "No, sadly, he won't."

"Oh, and he crapped himself, pardon my bluntness, so he was either scared shitless, as it were, or it's a result of strangulation. Urinated, too. Dry patches on his trousers, look."

His beige cargo pants bore the evidence of his accident, the edges of the stain reminding her of coastlines on maps. A pang of sorrow for him and how he'd felt during the attack threatened to swamp her for a moment, so she took a few deep breaths. Damon lingered nearby — close enough to hear, far enough away not to see everything in vivid detail, but she couldn't turn to him for a hug in the circumstances, a cuddle she badly needed.

"It's a tough job we do, isn't it?" Gilbert asked.

"Too tough at times — to the point you don't need added burdens."

"I hear you. Ignore him. Kane can be a mardy git sometimes. He's a great bloke underneath it, though. How would you feel in his shoes?" Gilbert asked gently.

"Pissed off, but I wouldn't go against the team leader. And I'm not just saying that because it suits me either. I wouldn't. I'd do my job, and if it all bothered me that much, I'd transfer somewhere else. That's why I came here. I didn't get on with the new chief, amongst other things, so I moved on."

"And will you move on again? From here, if Kane keeps up his behaviour?" He cocked his head and stood.

"Hell no."

"That's the spirit. Right, over here for a moment, please, if you will." He guided her to the side of the tent farthest from Kane. "This luckless victim—" he lowered his voice — "is a Colin Spinks."

Tracy whipped out her notebook.

"Driver's license has him at forty-one, and he lives at fifty-seven Starling Road. Now, I know you're new to this area, so here's the thing. He doesn't live far from here, and I'm not trying my hand at being a detective, but it doesn't take than much nous to realise he was either walking back home or possibly heading to town. From the car park, take a right out of the gates, then the next right. That's Starling Road. If you imagine it in your head, he was cutting through instead of walking around. Bet he wishes he hadn't now."

"Oh, stop it." She smiled. "You're awful."

"I know. Good, isn't it?" Gilbert guffawed. "Oh, and estimated time of death? Hard to say at the moment. The cold snap last night has messed with the body temp, and he's still in rigor, but that could also be late onset due to the cold. If the weather was warmer, he'd have been in and out of rigor by now if he'd been killed at, say, around eight o'clock last evening. Ah, the joys of my job, working out the maths."

"Someone would have seen him yesterday, surely, if he'd been killed earlier in the day."

"I dare say they would. People walk their dogs along this stream all the time, which is, incidentally, how he was spotted. The old dog-walker cliché. When I got here, the poor woman who'd discovered him was having kittens. Not literally, mind."

"I realise that . . ." She shook her head, damn lips quirking. "And she's where now?"

"Grumpy bollocks asked PC Newson to take a statement, and she's gone home. Out for a mid-morning walk, minding her own business, and the mutt started barking merry hell."

Tracy sighed. "Thanks. Well, I'll be off to visit the family, then — if he has any, that is. I'll get the woman's details from Newson — the dog walker's."

Gilbert smiled, nice and wide. "Righty ho. I'll be in touch when I discover more. And you take care of yourself. Don't let anyone—" he winked again — "get you down."

She shoved away images of Dr Schumer. "Oh, I don't intend to. I don't even plan on speaking to him at the moment." *Wonders will never cease.* "Thanks again for your kindness. Oh, I'll take the evidence of Colin's belongings back first." She took the bags he handed over, waved, and cocked her head at Damon, who trailed her out of the tent. "Let's keep our gear on until we get past the hedges. Saves Kane dobbing us in for contaminating a scene, the dick."

"I can't believe you actually blanked him," Damon said, his face pale with a hint of toad green about it. "You're getting better at this maturity thing."

"I'm trying. He isn't worth the hassle. I got myself all riled up, then saw that poor bastard bashed up in there — puts things in perspective. I'm going to find who did this, regardless of whether Kane tries to beat me to it or get in my way. If I ignore him, he might back off or, hopefully, disappear."

They reached the hedge, and Newson gave another sheepish smile.

"I need details of the woman who found the body," she said, smiling back. "Please don't give them to DI Barnett no matter how much he badgers you."

"I won't, ma'am."

He recited the name and address, and Tracy wrote it down.

"Thank you."

She nodded then bent and crab-walked under the tape. On the other side, she placed the evidence on the ground, removed her white gear, and rolled it into a ball. Damon did the same, then Tracy collected the bags, and they headed for the car park.

"I know I always say it, but I'll never get used to that sort of thing, Trace. The bodies."

"I know you won't, but you made progress this time. You didn't puke." She nudged him in the ribs. "And I have an ally. Gilbert."

"I heard."

"Do you think Kane did? Not that I'm bothered. I'd have said the same to his face. I think Gilbert would, too."

"Might not do him any harm to know his way of going about things isn't liked by everyone. I can understand his team sticking by him, though. They've probably worked with him for a long time. I imagine your guys back home — shit, not home anymore, but you know what I mean. They might be struggling to adapt to a new DI."

"Yes, but I'd like to think they'd be more mature about it. Anyway, enough of this bollocks. In the car. We need to get to . . . what's his name?" She peeked in her notebook. "Colin Spinks' place. Not what I thought we'd be doing when we started work this morning."

"Me neither."

After dropping the evidence back at the station, it didn't take long to get to Starling Road. Once Tracy had driven the route, she got her bearings a bit more and understood what Gilbert had been saying. It would chop a fair chunk of the journey off with Colin cutting through the park. Just another five or ten minutes added to his trip would see him at home or at work now, alive. She shook her head at the unfairness. Forty-one wasn't any age, was it, and she hoped he didn't have a wife and kids left behind, their world about to be devastated by her and Damon visiting. Then again, even if he wasn't married, he might have a girlfriend, mother, a father, brothers or sisters, so either way, someone was going to feel a whole heap of hurt.

"Here we are. Fifty-seven," she said and parked outside in the space between a rusty, old-fashioned red Renault and a brand-new silver Skoda.

The disturbing differences of life and status.

On the pavement, she waited for Damon, then led the way up the short garden path that appeared halfway to completion, the bed dug out and covered with sand, a clear plastic sheet over it, held in place by large stones, ready for either gravel or slabs. She imagined Colin working on it and ignored the twinge of sorrow that he'd never finish it. She couldn't be doing with getting upset — she didn't usually, so what was the deal now?

She knocked on the door and held her breath while taking out her warrant card. She glanced across at Damon, who, as usual, gave her a nod of support.

She had no idea what she'd do without him.

The door swung open, and there stood a woman in her late thirties, lacklustre blonde, a bit of a bird's nest sitting on top of her head in one of those trendy, messy buns. A dribbling brown-haired baby balanced on her hip, a piece of soggy toast squashed in its fist, melted butter shining on the fingers. No idea what sex it was; it only had a nappy on.

Shit.

"Hello?" the woman asked, frowning, her fashionable dark eyebrows almost joining above her nose. She appeared to have been crying, her cheeks pink-stained, her eyelids a tad puffy.

Of course, Colin hadn't come home last night . . .

"Hello. I'm DI Tracy Collier, and this is my colleague, DS Damon Hanks." Warrant card flash. "Is this the home of Colin Spinks?" Sensible to check. They could have split up, gone their separate ways, and he might not have changed his address with the DVLA yet.

"Yes. Is everything all right? Is Colin okay?" Her frown deepened, and she paled, clutching the baby tighter so it squirmed and let out a toast-muffled whine.

"Please could we come in?" Tracy asked, tilting her head and widening her eyes, silent communication that this really ought not to be done on the doorstep.

The woman moved back, and Tracy stepped inside, walking into the clean and tidy living room, the only mess a circle of neon-coloured toys on a black shaggy rug. The cream three-piece suite — no idea how it remained pristine with a child around. A large canvas hung on the back wall, the woman, the baby, and a man Tracy assumed was Colin, smiling, eyes alight with the glint of happiness.

Fucking hell's bells.

With everyone gathered, Tracy asked, "What's your name, love?" and berated herself for not phoning the station to find out first.

"Natasha. Is this about my Colin?"

"Are you Colin's wife?"

"Girlfriend. My surname is Moss. Look, you're worrying me. What's going on? Colin didn't come home last night, and I phoned the police to report it, but they said they couldn't do anything at the moment, that he could have just gone off for some alone time. But that isn't like Colin. He went out after work to town, to pick up some nappies for the baby, around six-thirty. He wouldn't have not brought them back. I had to borrow some off a neighbour after he didn't . . . come home."

Tracy thought back to the scene. She hadn't seen a packet of nappies.

Natasha bent to place the baby in a bouncy chair and strapped it in. The child's bottom lip wobbled, and tears formed, top lashes clumping together in spiky triangles. Natasha handed over a rattle. "There, Libby. Play with that for a minute."

A girl, then.

"Sit down, Natasha." Tracy locked any empathy away in order to get through this. She had to be frank, couldn't deliver news like this any other way, no matter how hard she tried, and when the woman sat, hands clasped in her lap, Tracy said, "I'm sorry to inform you that a body was found today, one we believe to be Colin."

Great delivery, as always.

Tracy cringed at herself. Natasha's mouth dropped open, and the most pain-filled wail came out of it, her features crumpling in slow motion. She raised her hands to clutch at her hair, the bun spilling to one side, a few tendrils coming loose. That set the baby off, and an identical screech joined her mother's, combining into a shriek of such desperate grief it had Tracy blinking.

I'm not crying. You are.

Damon did the gentlemanly thing and sat beside Natasha, resting a hand on her back. The poor cow leant into him, burrowing her face against his chest, and he looked up at Tracy, his expression so tortured she had to turn away.

Down on her knees, she unstrapped the screeching baby and picked it up, clueless as to how to handle a red-cheeked mini human who slapped her face with buttery hands, gums bright red, two bottom front teeth jutting out of it. She jiggled the child, humming a random tune, but the response she got wasn't the desired one. The baby cried harder.

"She needs you," Tracy said, stepping forward to pass the bundle to Natasha. And maybe by the woman holding her child it would centre her, give her a reason to focus on life rather than death.

Natasha eased away from Damon and held her hands out, sobbing while crushing her daughter to her, stroking her soft head.

And the wailing went on.

Unable to stand the emotion any longer, Tracy said, "Did Colin have a laptop or computer?"

"What?" Natasha stared, the terrible noise that had been coming out of her thankfully absent.

"A laptop?"

"Oh. Yes. There." Natasha pointed, and the moan of grief that poured between her lips was a heart-wrencher.

"Do you have anyone who can sit with you?" Tracy asked.

Natasha's noise abated slowly until she stared silently into the middle distance, face blank, as though nothing mattered and no information was getting into her head. Tracy understood that all too well. When Tracy had been faced with trauma in the Past, sometimes her mind and body had shut off for a few minutes, and she'd gazed absently into space, knowing the world was going on all around her but she'd been unable to participate.

Been there, done that.

"Anyone?" Tracy prompted.

"My . . . my mum. Lives round . . . the corner." Natasha hiccupped, and the baby finally, finally shut up. All right, it was grizzling quietly, but it was a damn sight better than the ear-splitting racket of before.

You're a heartless bitch, Tracy Collier.

She was, but she'd been made that way by events out of her control.

With the telephone number given, Tracy left the room to ring Natasha's mother in the kitchen with the door closed. She was treated to another long wail, sobs, and what sounded like the woman on the other end of the line staggering into a hard surface.

"Stay where you are," Tracy said. "I'm coming to pick you up."

Christ, this day needed to end already, but there were still Family Liaison officers to sort so they could sit with Natasha.

CHAPTER FIVE

Back at the station, Tracy handed in the laptop then set Nada and Lara the task of dealing with the CCTV in the town. They had a definite time of Colin leaving the house — six-thirty. If he'd walked to get nappies, he would have been caught on camera, and if he *hadn't* made it that far . . . But if he *had* managed to buy them, where were they now?

The park gates were closed at eight, so Tracy supposed Colin and the killer had entered before then on his way back, which narrowed down the hour of death. The killer would have needed to attack Colin before eight, too, in order to leave the park. Then again, there wasn't a gate blocking entry from the stream side, so they might have escaped via Starling Road.

She asked Tim to arrange house-to-house and join the uniformed officers there in questioning the residents in case anyone had seen a stranger enter the road between six forty-five and nine.

"What's that other copper's name? Used to be on Kane's team. Woman," she asked Damon while scrubbing Kane's writing off the whiteboard ready to add her own.

"Erica, I think," he said.

"Right, I'm going to get her back. With Kane God knows where, we need another body on the team." She wrote details down in capitals.

"What do you need me to do?"

"Ring Vic for me. That front desk bloke. Ask him where Erica's gone and locate her. I'll go and let Winter know she'll be back with us."

Once she'd finished adding info to the board, she hastened down the corridor. Outside Winter's office, she hesitated for a moment then knocked.

"Enter."

She popped her head around the door. "Got a moment, sir?"

"Ah, yes. Come in, Tracy." He immediately got up and walked to the coffee machine, jaunty, as though an excuse for a brew was what he'd been waiting for.

"Just an update, sir, before we get really busy and I might not have time to check in with you." She sat and made herself comfortable, crossing one leg over the other.

"I'm not the type to pester for information," he said, "but I appreciate the thought. I prefer to work along the lines of if you have something to report, you'll do so, otherwise, get on with it. That suit you?"

"Most definitely. I hate being chased. Adds pressure, and with an investigation like this, I need to be focused, not thinking about having to come to you every five minutes."

"Then we'll get along just fine." He handed her a coffee then sat behind his desk with his. "On you go, then."

"First, and most important, the body this morning was definitely murder."

"Christ." He sighed. "Okay."

"I've informed the next of kin. CCTV is being checked, house-to-house actioned. I won't bore you with the details. I'll be visiting the dog walker who found the victim shortly. Second, Kane was at the scene before me, as we suspected. Unfortunate that he seems to want to dig a hole for himself, but there you go. I hate to have to say this—" *I don't really* — "but from what I gathered from PC Newson, Kane had claimed the scene, and it *seems* as though he purposely sowed seeds to keep me out." She scowled. "I ended up having to ask Newson to telephone Vic Atkins to verify who I am. Not good." She pursed her lips, keeping back a multitude of swear words.

"Oh dear."

"Indeed. I declined to speak to Kane at the scene, despite him giving me dirty looks, as though he wanted to goad me, and concentrated on the victim and gathering information from Gilbert. That's what I'm paid to do, not argue with some tosser." She shrugged. "Sorry, sir. Anyway, as you can see, I'm back, but Kane isn't. I have no idea where he is or what he's doing, and frankly, I don't give a monkey's. Gilbert didn't give Kane any victim information, so I can only hope he hasn't found it out some other way and is visiting Natasha Moss — the victim's girlfriend — all over again." She sighed and rubbed her forehead, a slight headache coming on. "This is why I made my speech earlier about only me leading this team. Too many cooks and all that. Kane could upset a lot of people if he's doubling up on visits and whatnot. So, third, as Kane isn't about, I need Erica back. I can't expect the others to handle this with a man down if Kane is playing silly buggers." She took a warming sip of coffee, and it burned all the way down her windpipe. Something else to think about for a second.

Winter shook his head and harrumphed. "See, this is what I don't understand. I told you Kane's former partner, Richard, died. Cancer, hanged himself, terrible business. But when Richard received his final prognosis, the man went off the rails a bit. Understandably so, too. Can't imagine what the poor devil went through. He didn't particularly participate in the investigation they were working on at the time, and Kane had to cope by himself when Richard went AWOL. Now, I distinctly recall Kane coming in here and having a bit of a rage over it. So why, then, does he feel it's okay to do the same to you? He's effectively doing a Richard and is unavailable. Do as I do, don't do as I say?"

"Sounds like it." Tracy shrugged. Winter talking about Kane being in the same boat as her with regards to a team member not pulling his weight rankled her. "This coffee, sir. Got to be the best I've had."

He beamed. "Yes, love it myself, too. Wonderful brand, available on Amazon. I'll give you the link to it sometime."

"Please, otherwise I might have to bother you with more regular updates until you do." She laughed, a smidgen of tension floating away, easing the stabbing pain in her neck that had arisen with all that talk about Kane.

"Uh, that won't be necessary. The coffee stays in the carafe from now on when you're in here. The link — it's yours straight after you walk out of that door there."

She chuckled again. "Seriously now, what do we do about Kane?"

"Well, he's defied orders and gone missing without reporting to you. He'll have to be spoken to about that — leave that side of it to me. Possibly a written warning needs doling out, although I'm reluctant to do that because he's been exemplary up until now. However, I have to stick by the rules, I suppose. Let's see. I'll insist he takes time off, a cooling down period where he gets the chance to assess what he wants to do — stay on this team or go elsewhere. If he stays, he behaves, no leeway on that. I'll be incredibly upset to lose him if he decides to try his hand somewhere else, but the serious crimes squad is too important for him to mess it up just because he's got it into his head he isn't vital enough, or valued enough, to lead it for me. That's my take on it, anyway. So, as of this moment, he's off the squad until we can work out what the hell's going on. Inform your team again — and Vic — that under no circumstances must Kane be given any more information regarding this murder. He's the type to go rogue, by the way, and try to solve it alone. Prove a point that he should be running the shop."

"Hmm, I thought the same. Okay, thank you. I'm going to settle Erica in then get back out there with Damon to talk to the dog walker. Maybe she saw the packet of nappies."

"Nappies?" His eyebrows shot up.

"Doesn't matter. Something to do with the case." She sipped more of her drink. "God, I need to abduct your packet of coffee."

He chortled, and they finished their drinks in silence, Tracy contemplating the absence of Kane, hoping he wasn't screwing anything up. Maybe she should talk to him when he finally showed his face. As a friend, not a colleague. She couldn't shake the feeling there was more to his behaviour than her turning up this morning and upending his career.

"Right," she said, rising and taking her cup to the filing cabinet. "I'll be in touch when anything significant happens. Thanks for the coffee and the support."

"No problem whatsoever. Good luck."

She nodded and left the room, closing the door then heading for the incident room. Still no Kane, but Erica sat at her old desk, writing notes on a pad.

"Hi," Tracy said. "Great to have you back. I'd like you to dig into Colin Spinks' background for me — getting you up to speed, he's the murder victim. The usual needs finding — any previous, family members, friends, you know the drill. We need to look for anything dodgy, or any arguments in the past that may have resulted in someone wanting to do him harm. I've broken the news to his girlfriend, but I will need to speak to other relations to build a broader picture of him. If you can do that by the end of the day, that would be amazing and very much appreciated. And I'll just repeat — no going through Kane." She handed Erica her card. "Both my mobile numbers are on there. You get hold of me any time. The chief is well aware of Kane's . . . behaviour, and anyone following suit will be issued a written warning." She smiled brightly. "So best you don't go down the same path as him, eh? Oh, and I'm really not that much of a bitch once you get to know me, I promise. You look after me, I'll look after you, understand?"

Erica nodded and grinned somewhat reluctantly. If the woman wanted to be iffy with Tracy, she could get on with it — so long as she did her job.

Tracy left Erica and went to stand in front of the whiteboard. "If I could just have your attention for a minute, everyone. Sorry, I know you're all busy. Pause that CCTV footage a second, will you, Nada? Thanks." She pressed her hands together and held them at waist height. "Now, I'm not purposely Kane bashing, I swear, but please, for the length of this investigation, do *not* give him any information — Winter's orders, so for the love of God, don't go against what he's said. Kane is off the squad for now because of defying me, visiting a crime scene without permission, and now he's off somewhere or other doing whatever it is he's bloody doing. He's unaware of being off the squad, so please don't say a word until Winter has informed him. As you know, that's a written warning offence — possibly worse. So, as I just said to Erica: Don't go down the same path."

Nada raised her finger. "Do you want me to talk to him? Kane, I mean."

"Um, up to you, but obviously not about this case or him not being on it. Anyone found leaking information . . . well, you get the drift. If there's something other than me leading this team bothering him, by all means, try to get it out of him. Otherwise, steer clear so you don't get dragged down into the shit pit with him." Tracy looked at each team member in turn. "All clear?"

Several nods and a couple of indecipherable murmurs. Going by the tone, they weren't negative.

Thank God for small mercies.

"Okay, brilliant. Damon and I are off to the dog walker's. Tomorrow, we'll need to speak to Natasha Moss again — Colin Spinks' girlfriend. She wasn't fit for interviewing today. Now, my mobile numbers are on the top of that whiteboard there. All info gathered so far is also on that board. I'm going to turn it round now so if Kane returns, he can't clock any details. Sounds ridiculous for us to be behaving this way, but it's his own stupid fault. Right, off to work then, and I'll be back soon. Anything significant comes in, call me immediately. Oh, and don't forget to have lunch." She fished in her pocket and drew out a twenty. "Here." She slapped it on Nada's desk. "Buy sandwiches or something to eat at your desks — sorry, no time for a proper break today. Nada, I'm leaving it up to you to inform Winter if Kane comes back in. Do it via phone or text if it makes it less obvious what you're up to. See you later, guys." She waved. "Damon, you're with me."

CHAPTER SIX

Notes:
When they look like the person you really despise, it's easier to get rid of them. Strength comes from hate and fuels the mission.

The first man resembled *him* so much I'd thought for a second it *was* him. When I'd followed him into the park, him swinging a bag of Pampers by his side, he'd glanced at me over his shoulder once we'd got past the gap in the hedges, probably checking to see if I was anyone worth worrying about, some big beefy bloke, out to do him harm. All he'd seen was me, and he'd waved then carried on, giving a little shrug, probably thinking: *She's just taking a shortcut home.*

Wrong.

Well, he'd found that out soon enough, hadn't he?

Twat.

I'd whacked him on the back of his head at first, see, to get his attention, let him know I meant business. He'd gathered that, what with the *ow* and *oomph* that had come out of him, and he'd spun around, hand on the wound, eyes narrowed, bloody great big frown on his overly long forehead. You could park a car on it.

"What the fuck?" he'd said, all bullish and aggressive, when really, there hadn't been any need to be so rude. "What's your game?"

"Game?" I'd said. "I'm not playing a game here, I'm being deadly serious."

I keep chuckling now at that phrase. *Deadly* serious. Deary me.

He'd gone for me then, you know, darted forward to take away my weapon, but I'd lunged at him, bringing it down on the front of his skull. Made a nice cracking sound, it did, and that was it, he went south like a sack of shit, on his knees, begging me not to hit him again, mumbling about having a baby who needed the nappies he'd bought. Like I didn't know that. His voice had been slurred, and it annoyed me. I remember this rage bursting inside me, and I thought of *him* and all the times *he'd* slurred after having one of those sodding asthma attacks of his.

That did it, really. I'd bashed the living daylights out of him then, four or five more wallops on his head, much easier with him kneeling like that, I have to say. But the git had got up, staggering along beside the stream, weaving left and right and at one point almost pitching into the water. I'd stood there, staring in amazement that with such extensive wounds, with his brain peeking out to say hello, he was actually walking away after a fashion.

That got me angrier, and I'd stalked after him, weapon raised, and he'd turned a few yards away, maybe to check if I was following. Blood had streaked down his face, and his eyes, they'd gone wider the closer I'd got. He'd moved backwards and must have caught his heel on a stone or whatever — clumsy bastard, but to be fair, the ground is a bit rough down there — and he'd toppled, landing on his arse.

By the time I'd reached him, wheezing gusts had whooshed out of his slack mouth. Wet lips. Can't abide them. One more smack to the head, and I'd thrown my weapon down, dived on him until his back met the ground, and I sat on him, hands around his throat. So many times

I'd envisaged doing that to *him*, and last night I'd taken such pleasure in acting out the fantasy. Squeezing a throat aided by years of pent-up anger is such a satisfying endeavour, and I can't wait to do it again.

Afterwards, at home, I wasn't best pleased about having to clean my weapon. The water had turned pink, and as it had swirled down the drain, it left streaks, a few hairs, and a red lump or two in the bottom of the sink. I'd poked them down the plughole.

I suppose I'll have to get used to that side of things, won't I.

Is it too soon to go out again this evening? I'll admit I have a taste for it now, and it'll be interesting to see if last night's episode repeats itself this time or whether it'll be completely different.

Hmm.

Thinking of all that blood reminds me. I need to put my clothes in the washing machine now they've had a good soak in cold salty water. And I need to check that packet of nappies for any red smears or dirt. He'd flung them in the air on my second strike, and when I'd left him there, I'd clocked they were the same size as *his* youngest uses. Waste not, want not. They'll come in handy for that little brat, no doubt about it.

* * *

The Past

We married on a bright and sunny Friday in the registry office, my friends as bridesmaids, Beryl the chief of them all. Alfie was fine with me having three, and besides, he knows them very well. We all work for him in the secretarial pool.

I still go to work, and I will until I'm pregnant. Alfie says no mother of his children will need to earn any money, and I'm so excited to be able to stay at home and raise our babies. We'll have three or four, and perhaps, when they're a little older, we'll get a puppy for them to play with.

All my friends are married now, too, but they've opted to expand their families once they've saved enough for down payments on houses and have secured mortgages. They have it all mapped out, just like me.

Things are going to be wonderful, aren't they?

* * *

We've been trying for a year, and still no baby. I've talked to Beryl about it, and she's admitted she would like a baby now, too, but her husband insists on using condoms, as do our other friends' husbands. Us four girls are so ready to begin the next phase of our lives, but it seems only Alfie is on board. Their other halves are adamant that the children won't come for a few years.

Beryl is here to console me. There's a work party later; Alfie arranged it as an end-of-tax-year bash. I can't go. A bug has hit me, and it has affected my tummy. I'm throwing up every so often, and I tell Beryl it's best she leaves so she doesn't catch whatever it is I've got.

"Could you be pregnant?" she asks, eyes wide.

I widen mine, too. I hadn't even thought me being sick could be that. *"Of course I could be. Alfie has been trying very hard to get me pregnant. Oh God, it would be so wonderful, wouldn't it?"*

Beryl sighs. "I can't wait until it's my turn. I feel it's time, but I don't think it's in my immediate future."

* * *

Alfie stumbles into the bedroom after the party, stinking of alcohol and staggering as he removes his clothes. The smell has me retching again, and I rush to the bathroom to empty my stomach.

When I return to the bedroom, Alfie is fast asleep, snoring.

I'm wide awake, so I pop on the bedside lamp and think I'll have a bit of a read.

In bed, I look across at Alfie. His back is to me, and on that back are scratches so deep it appears he's been in a fight. I lean over to check his face, and scratches are there, too, as though someone raked their nails down his cheek. It isn't like Alfie to get into a physical confrontation.

He's good with words and verbally negotiating himself out of anything remotely argumentative.

Panic flutters in my chest. What happened at that party? I think about the employees at work, and only one of the junior accountants strikes me as having a temper. Did he and Alfie fall out? Then again, the get-together had been held at a posh hotel, and any altercations would have been dealt with swiftly by security.

Wouldn't they?

I don't know, and I don't want to read now.

I switch the light out and stare into the dark, my mind whirling.

CHAPTER SEVEN

In the living room belonging to Miss Fiona Owens — a slim, twenty-something preppy sort, black cropped hair, tortoise-shell-framed glasses, blue eyes — Tracy perched on a red-and-cream-checked wingback chair while Damon sat beside the dog walker on the cherry-hued sofa, notebook in hand. The pup sprawled across Fiona's feet, a mixed breed, coat the colour of wet sand and just as coarse by the look of it.

"So you left the house at what time?" Tracy asked, elbows on her knees, dangling her hands in the triangle between her legs.

"Um, had to have been around . . . tennish? Yes, got to have been, because I remember checking the clock in the kitchen to see if I could make it back in time before the sausages were done. I'd put them in the oven on low. As I live two streets over from Starling Road, it takes about ten minutes to get to the alley there that leads to the stream."

Alley. Interesting. That's our next stop.

"Another ten minutes to get to where you found him, would you say?" Tracy enquired.

"More like fifteen. So I must have found him about twenty-five past or thereabouts."

"And you saw no other people around on your walk?"

"Unusually, no. We normally bump into at least two other people with dogs on our first outing of a morning, but today, nothing."

"I see. So your dog found him first, yes?"

She nodded. "Zoom — that's my dog's name — galloped off ahead then stopped and sniffed what I thought was a pile of clothing or a tramp asleep on the bank. It's not uncommon for the homeless to camp there — it's out of the way, although the ones I've seen in the past have pop-up tents, believe it or not. Got them from some charity-based place in town. Such a great idea."

Tracy smiled, eager to steer the convo away from tents and the kindness of people dishing them out. "What happened then?"

"I walked over to see what Zoom was up to and . . . Oh God . . ." She pressed a hand to her chest. "I realised it was a man, but his face . . ."

"Yes, it was a sight, wasn't it, and I'm sorry you had to see that," Tracy said.

"Oh, I'll never forget it. I think it'll haunt me for years."

"I can imagine. Then what?"

"I used my mobile and rang nine-nine-nine. I moved away from the—" she shuddered — "body as I was instructed to but stayed close enough to warn anyone else if they came along. No one did, and the dispatcher asked me to check for a pulse, so I had to tie Zoom up to a branch using his lead, but the second I touched the man's neck . . ." She retched and flapped her hand midair, her face flushing deep red. "He was so hard and . . . ugh . . . cold, that I . . . screamed, and I got dried blood on my fingers." She heaved again. "Sorry. I keep seeing it in my head and thinking about all the . . . blood."

"Damon can sympathise with you there, Fiona." Tracy widened her eyes at him.

"Yes," he said. "I can't stomach seeing them like that either. I'm struggling with you talking about it, to be honest, so don't mind me if I start gagging as well."

Fiona laughed somewhat uneasily, and Tracy winked at Damon in thanks for stopping the woman from having a meltdown.

"So, moving on . . . You gave a statement to a PC Newson, I believe?" Tracy said.

"Yes, but before that, a man called Barnacle or something."

Tracy choked back laughter. "Barnett."

"Yes, that's it." Fiona bobbed her head several times. "I told him what had happened, and he gave me his card, saying if I thought of anything else, I should contact him. Then he told me to give my details to the other policeman. Newton."

"Newson."

"Sorry, I'm so muddled. It's like my brain isn't working properly." She paled then shot from her seat and out into the hallway, Zoom scrabbling after her, skidding on the laminate flooring to the point Tracy thought he would do himself some damage.

A door slammed, then came the sound of her vomiting.

"I think that's enough now, don't you?" Damon said quietly.

"Yes, most definitely. She didn't see anyone else around, so it's pointless asking more questions."

"Right."

Fiona returned, her skin damp with a sheen of sweat, and lowered herself onto the sofa. The dog jumped onto her lap, whining and pressing his nose into the crook of her neck.

It's got more compassion than me . . .

Tracy stood, as did Damon.

"Here's my card." Tracy handed it to her. "Please don't contact Barnacle."

Fiona chuckled despite her obvious distress. "So sorry about calling him that."

"Don't worry. I found it funny. He's not on the case anymore, so it's me you need to speak to, all right? If you require any help, anyone to talk to, ring me using either of the numbers on my card, and I'll offer you contact details where you can speak to people trained in dealing with your type of trauma. Even if you think you're okay, the memories can come back to bite you in the behind at a later date, believe me, so if you need help months down the line, don't hesitate to get in touch."

They took their leave and, out on the pavement beside the car, Tracy said, "We need to look at that alley. Plus, we can pop in on Tim, see how the house-to-house is going. That'll need to be repeated later when people are home from work, I'll bet. They might not be getting much of a response at this time of day." She checked her watch. "Well past lunchtime. We need to nip somewhere to get food after seeing that alley."

They drove back to Starling Road, and after checking in with Tim — so far, the residents at home hadn't seen anyone or heard anything, what a surprise — they walked to the alley. Between two houses midway down the street, it led to a field, a path cutting through the middle of it.

"Fancy a walk, do you?" Tracy asked.

"Needs must." Damon shrugged.

At the end of the field, trees stood in a line either side of the path, and a small wooden bridge arched over the stream. Something flapped in the breeze, stuck to one of the bridge rail posts. Tracy moved closer. It was a piece of Asda sticky tape, usually attached to things that didn't fit into carrier bags, with a receipt Sellotaped to it.

"Got a baggie?" she asked.

Damon produced one while she pulled gloves out of her pocket and put them on. Then she took the baggie.

"This is a receipt for *nappies.*" She put the evidence in the bag and sealed the top.

"You what?" Damon had a look. "Fucking hell. So he *did* get to the supermarket — and it'd be a massive coincidence if this wasn't his receipt. Says time of purchase, six-fifty."

"So he was killed on his way home," she said, putting the bag in her jacket pocket. "Christ Almighty, that poor sod."

"I know. And someone had to have found the nappies and walked this way with them."

"Bastard." She sighed out her anger, taking the gloves off so she could dial the incident room. "That you, Nada? That CCTV, skip to the camera outside Asda. Think you'll find Colin Spinks went there. We'll be back soon. Bye." Then to Damon, "Let's get this bit over and done with so we can take this evidence to the station for processing."

They crossed the bridge, and, on the other side, Tracy took the lead until the forensic tent came into view.

"Right, I've got the layout cemented in my head now," she said. "And I'm not going down to the tent again in case that prat is still there. Back to the car then."

In Starling Road, she was about to get into her vehicle when Tim waved and ran over.

"Boss, a passerby saw something — someone — but I don't think it's significant. Thought I'd tell you anyway."

"What's that then?" She offered him an encouraging smile.

"A lady in number twelve — an Alison Imers — said she saw an old lady . . . well, old to her, she said. Late sixties, something like that. Reckons it's some old dear who usually walks past in the morning. Alison thinks she goes to the local shop at the end of the road there to get a newspaper. Anyway, the old lady lives in Robin's Way — all the roads on this estate are birds, see — number twenty-one. Hilda Jones. Alison knows this because she went to school with Mrs Jones' neighbour's son — a Francis Vale — and visited for tea there when she was about twelve. What bothered Alison is that the woman was hobbling, using a walking stick, and she thought she might be hurt. Should one of us go round and check she's okay?"

Tracy held back a sigh. "We'll do it now. Thanks."

Tim nodded then returned to talk to a PC.

"It'll be dinnertime before we get any lunch at this rate," Tracy grumbled along with her stomach.

"Well, if the team have to eat at their desks, then we should eat on the go, too."

"But at least they've probably eaten by now. My gut's protesting. I'm caved-over hungry, know what I mean?"

"Caved over?" Damon frowned.

"You know, you could just bend over because the pain is a bit much in your belly."

"Can't say I've ever experienced that, but . . . Let's get to Mrs Jones' then find a sandwich place."

They left Starling Road and didn't have a problem finding Robin's Way — it was the same street Fiona Owens lived in. At Mrs Jones', Tracy rang the bell and waited, Damon a pace or two behind her on the path. The door opened, and far from seeing a hunched, wizened elderly lady, weak as a kitten, a robust, large-framed woman filled the doorframe, her cheeks ruddy, a bit of a bruise on her cheek, her more-salt-than-pepper hair scraped back into a severe bun at her nape.

Miss Trunchbull, anyone?

"Yes?" she demanded, her voice deep and a tad alarming — hoarse from years of nicotine or perhaps a recent spell of shouting.

"DI Tracy Collier and DS Damon Hanks." Tracy showed her identification. "We've just nipped by to see if you're all right."

"Ha! Are you police doing community calls now or something? Thought there'd been budget cuts." She sniffed. "Of *course* I'm all right. Who says I'm not?" She curled her hands into fists then plonked them on her hips.

Bloody Nora . . .

"A neighbour saw you struggling with a walking stick last night," Tracy said.

"A walking stick? Haven't got one of those. And struggling? *Struggling*? I do *not* damn well struggle. I'm as sprightly as you like, thank you very much, and I don't appreciate people saying otherwise."

"Sorry about that, Mrs Jones, just following up on someone's concern. You should be grateful people care." *What is she like?*

"They should mind their own," she said, tapping the side of her globular nose. "Like I do." She made to close the door.

"Uh, just a moment, Mrs Jones." Tracy held a hand up. "Where did you get that bruise on your face?"

"I tripped over while going up the stairs."

"Being too sprightly, were you?"

"Why, you . . ."

"What were you doing in Starling Road last night?"

"Starling bleeding Road?" She squinted, staring at something above Tracy's head, possibly Damon. "I was nowhere near the sodding place. I was in here, wasn't I, watching my soap."

"I see. What soap was that?"

"*Eastenders*, seven-thirty sharp until eight, then after that I went to bed early."

"I see. So you wouldn't have seen anyone out and about in this street then?"

"What do you take me for, a nosy beak? No, I didn't see anyone 'out and about' as you put it. Why would I care if anyone's 'out and about'? I've got better things to do with my time."

"All right, Mrs Jones. It's just that I'm confused as to why someone swears they saw you — and they know you — yet you're saying you weren't there."

"Oh, so you'll believe someone else over me, will you? Charming, that is. I know your game, trying to trap me into saying what you want. Well, it won't work. I wasn't out, I was here, so stick that in your pipe and chuff on it until smoke comes out of your arse."

She slammed the door.

Tracy turned to face Damon. "What the actual fuck did we just witness there?"

"A crotchety, rude old bag. Alison Imers was probably mistaken. It was dark. People see what they think they see, not what's actually there." Damon went back down the path and waited for her on the pavement.

"But . . ." Tracy scowled. "Oh, fuck it. The station, then food. If I don't eat soon, I'm likely to start getting ratty."

She joined him, and they walked back to the car.

"Start?" he said. "*Start* getting ratty?"

She glanced over the roof at him from the driver's side. His grin broke up the retort sitting on her tongue. "Oh, be quiet, you."

Laughing, they got in and headed back to the station.

With the receipt and sticker evidence handed in, Damon went up to the incident room, while Tracy legged it to a nearby shop and bought prepacked sandwiches — only egg mayonnaise and cress left, bugger it. She returned to the station and handed Damon his butty while scoping out the desks to see if Kane had returned.

He hadn't.

Then she said to everyone, "I need to eat this and take five — head's spinning — then I'll come out to update you and see what you've found, if anything."

CHAPTER EIGHT

Her break short and sweet — there was something to be said about being alone for five or ten minutes to regroup, even if the sandwich she'd eaten was damn gross and soggy — Tracy entered the incident room ready to go again, energised and with a new purpose.

Her phone rang in her pocket, but she ignored it.

"Right." She brought them up to date with the Asda tape/receipt find, the grouchy old bat in Robin's Way, and the statement given by Fiona Owens. "So, Nada, how did the Asda CCTV search go?"

"I think we've spotted him, boss. The guys at the CCTV control room sent this over after I rang them — we'd been looking at the other files they'd provided earlier, located closer to the park," Nada said and moved her monitor so it faced the middle of the room. She accessed the file, played it, and fast-forwarded. "There he is." She paused it, brought his face up larger, then tapped the screen with a knuckle. "If I reduce this box here a second and pull up his driver's licence photo . . . There, see? I reckon it's definitely him, don't you?"

"Looks very likely. What time is he entering the shop there?" Tracy asked, the numbers at the bottom of the box too small to make out from where she stood by the whiteboard.

"Twelve minutes past seven, which ties in with him leaving home at six-thirty," Nada said. "Then he goes into Asda and leaves at seventeen minutes past — so literally a quick shop then out again. He has a packet of Pampers."

"The Asda sticker is flapping, look," Tracy said, "so it wasn't stuck completely down the length of the nappy bag." She resisted punching the air — if fingerprints came off that tape or the receipt of someone other than Asda workers and Colin Spinks, at least they'd have a lead. It just meant they'd have to match the prints to someone. "Right, Nada, go to Asda and find out which till he chose, who served him, and get an estimate of how many people might have touched that tape prior to it being used so we know how many potential sets of fingerprints we need to take. And . . . Oh. Shit . . ." She remembered something. "I have to go. Keep doing what you're doing, Erica. Damon, we need to seriously get a move on."

Heart pounding at her absolutely horrendous mistake, she raced to the car park, Damon chasing after her and calling out, "What the hell's going on, Trace?"

She waited until they were in the car to tell him. "Colin Spinks has a *girlfriend*, not a wife, right?"

"Yes . . ." His expression blank, he said, "So . . ."

"She's not his proper next of kin, as it were. We didn't inform his parents of his death." She rubbed her hands over her face. "*I* didn't inform them, I should say — it's not your fault." She phoned Vic so her team wouldn't be aware of her incompetence. She didn't need them to know she was only human so soon after starting with the squad. "Vic, Tracy Collier here. Quick as you can, an address for the parents of a Colin Spinks, fifty-seven Starling Road. No, I'll wait." She eyed Damon, cheeks flushing so hot they itched. "I could kick myself, Damon," she whispered. "I messed up before in the city as well, us watching that pizza delivery bloke on the last case thinking he was the killer when he pissing well wasn't. I blamed that on not getting proper time off, a break, but I can't blame this fuck-up on anyone but myself. I'm so damn cross!"

"Don't . . . This murder came out of nowhere."

"Eh? What are you on, man? They all do, don't they?"

"You know what I mean. We weren't expecting one on our first day. There's been a lot to do. And don't forget, you were waylaid by Tim and having to go and see that rude old cow in Robin's Way, then the alley . . . You've realised now, so that's the main thing."

"Here's hoping Natasha Moss doesn't like her would-have-been mother-in-law and she hasn't rung or gone to see her yet." She held up a finger. "Right, thanks, Vic." She cut the call. "I don't believe it. Back to bloody Robin's Way." She started the car and headed off.

"You're joking!"

"Do I look like I'm laughing? No, I'm not — face, no smile. We're going to be sick of that street by the time this case is finished." She took a hard left and put her foot down.

"What number is it?"

"Never mind the number. We know exactly where it is. It's next door to that ruddy old battle-axe's house."

"You *what*?"

"Yep."

"Jesus . . ." He laughed. "Sod's law, this is."

"I know."

They made it in good time, and at Mrs Spinks' front door, Tracy steeled herself for possibly getting a dressing down from the woman if Natasha had opened her mouth already. Tracy deserved it, too.

"Back again?"

Tracy recognised that mannish voice and turned to her right. Hilda Jones stood on her doorstep in an old-fashioned blue-and-white-striped house coat with a gaudy, flowery apron tied around her waist. So much for her not being a nosy beak.

"Yes?" Tracy snapped. "Can I help you?"

"Not really." Mrs Jones hefted up her ample bosom with her folded arms. "Just that you came to see me earlier, then another copper came and stood right where you are, and now you're back and all."

"Another copper?" *If Kane's been here, I'll . . .* "Describe the police officer, please."

"A bloke."

That helps immensely, you awkward . . . Don't say it, Tracy. "A bloke. Right. If you don't mind, would you please go inside?"

"No. Free country." She sniffed and looked down her nose at Tracy. "I can stand on my doorstep all the live-long day if I so choose. And I choose."

Tracy stopped herself from closing her eyes in frustration. She didn't want to give the woman the satisfaction of knowing she was getting right on her nellies. "Whatever, love." She waved a hand in dismissal.

"Whatever, love? What*ever*, love? Why, you're rude and no mistake. I should report you. I remember your name, too, Tracy Collier. And you, Damon poncy Banks."

"Hanks," Damon said.

"That's what I said," Mrs Jones huffed.

"No, you said *Banks*," Tracy corrected. *So help me God, but I'm going to swing for her in a minute.*

"Ignore her," Damon whispered close to her ear. "We're here to do a job, not give her something to occupy her time."

Tracy knocked on Mrs Spinks' door.

"Don't you know it's rude to whisper?" Mrs Jones said. "Didn't your mother teach you any manners?"

"My mother taught me fine enough," Damon said, him with the patience of a saint.

"No, she didn't." Mrs Jones smirked. "Not if you're whispering when in company."

Tracy's temper snapped. "Didn't your mother teach you to *fuck off* when you aren't wanted?" *Oh God. Well done, Collier.*

"Oh, I say!" Mrs Jones' face reddened. "I'll be reporting you."

"I'll be denying it," Tracy snarled.

"So will I," Damon said.

Bless his heart.

The front door opened, and Tracy switched her catty, childish head for her professional one. "Mrs Spinks?"

The woman had been crying — *shit, she's already been told.* Her grey hair a fluffy halo, the wrinkles on her cheeks clogged with beige powder, she resembled most people's gran.

"Yes?" She dabbed a tissue to her eye.

"What's the matter, Beryl?" Mrs Jones moved off her step to lean over the waist-high wooden fence separating their gardens.

Hope she gets splinters in her tits.

"DI Tracy Collier and Damon *Hanks*," Tracy said, giving Jones a pointed stare. "Please may we come in?"

Beryl Spinks allowed them entry and closed the door. "Are you here again about me going out last night?" She squeezed the tissue like a stress ball. "Or is it about Colin? Is he all right? Have you found where he got to? I can't imagine why he wouldn't have come home. Him and Natasha are getting married in two months, and he's so happy about it, so there's no reason he would have gone off like that."

"Can we go and sit down, Mrs Spinks?" Tracy asked.

"Gawd, yes, so sorry. This way." She shuffled into the kitchen and gestured to the pine table and chairs. "A policeman came earlier, a Tim someone or other. He had plain clothes on, but he showed me ID like you did, so I let him in. I did the right thing, didn't I? Please, park your backsides."

Tim? What the hell was he doing here? If he's working with Kane . . .

Tracy and Damon sat beside each other, opposite Beryl.

"Yes, Tim is a policeman, it's fine, Mrs Spinks. What did he want?" Tracy asked.

"Well, I thought he'd come here to give me news about Colin. The policeman has not long gone, to be honest. About twenty minutes ago he came. But it wasn't about Colin. He wanted to know what I was doing in Starling Road last night — someone had seen me there — but I'd gone out to look for my son, see, that's what I was doing, and when he asked me what my son's name was and I told him, he went awfully pale."

Tracy let out a breath slowly. "So he questioned you about being in Starling Road. Okay. And he didn't say anything about Colin?"

"No, he left once I told him why I was in that street. He looked like he wanted to be sick, and I thought maybe he was coming down with something in the belly department, you know, because Colin gets like that when he isn't very well, so I advised him to take some Alka Seltzer. For the trots or a tummy ache, you see."

Tracy had the absurd urge to cry.

This poor woman, worrying about someone being poorly when her life is about to be turned upside down.

"Two seconds." Tracy swallowed the lump in her throat and pulled her phone out of her pocket. A missed call from Tim.

Fuck, so he'd tried to tell me he'd been here.

Phone away, she composed herself and said, "Mrs Spinks, it is with regret that I have to inform you—"

"Oh God, no. Not my boy. Please don't tell me my boy's gone. Not my Colin." She slapped a hand to her chest. "He only went out for nappies. How can something happen to you when you just go out for nappies? There must be some mistake. That's what it is, a mistake." She stared at Tracy, eyes swimming, bottom lip wobbling. "Isn't it?" she whispered.

"I'm afraid not, Mrs Spinks." *Hate my job.* "Is there anyone I can call to sit with you?"

"I . . . Hilda next door. She's my friend." Mrs Spinks flushed. "What happened? To Colin?" Her face was near white, and tears spilled. She had the look about her of someone not quite believing what they'd heard, as though the other shoe hadn't dropped, and when it did, she'd be a wreck.

"Um, I'm so sorry," Tracy said, "but he was murdered."

"Murdered? Oh, dear God . . . His dad . . . his dad was murdered. This can't be happening again." She sucked in a huge breath, but it didn't come out again. Her eyes rolled, and a choking noise gurgled past her lips.

"Shit, Damon, she's . . ."

Mrs Spinks toppled to the side, hitting the chair next to her, then she smacked onto the lino.

"Call an ambulance," Damon said. "I'll deal with her."

Heart hammering wildly, Tracy dashed into the hallway and made the call, memories of having to ring for paramedics when she'd found Damon half dead flashing through her mind. She lost the ability to breathe for a moment, the recollection stark and unforgiving. The dispatcher repeated herself, asking which service Tracy required. She managed to get the words out then returned to the kitchen.

"I'm a police officer, another officer is giving mouth to mouth."

Damon quickly glanced at her and shook his head.

"There's no sign of life," Tracy said.

Then Damon breathed air into her again, and Mrs Spinks' eyelids fluttered.

"She's back," Damon said, placing his ear near her face. "Breath on my cheek. Oh, thank fuck . . ."

The paramedics arrived quickly, and after Mrs Spinks had been taken away, Tracy had it in mind to reach over the fence and knock on Mrs Jones' door, but the infernal woman was at her gate, staring after the departing ambulance.

"Mrs Jones, as you're Beryl's friend, do you have a key for her house?" Tracy asked.

Mrs Jones turned and stomped up her path, one bottom corner of her apron lifting, the flowers on it seeming to dance as though kissed by a summer breeze. "What's it to you, Tracy Collier?"

The woman's repetition of her name wasn't lost on Tracy.

"Beryl will need to be able to return home, and as she didn't take a key with her, seeing as she was in no fit state to remember she'd need one . . ." Tracy glared at her.

"Yes, yes, I have a key. I have keys for all my closest neighbours. What's up with her, anyway?"

Tracy wouldn't usually say anything, but the need to shock this hateful woman pushed her to opening her mouth. "She seems to have had a heart attack because her son was killed last night."

Mrs Jones' mouth gaped. "Her son was killed? Colin?"

"Yes." *So stick that in your pipe and chuff on it until smoke comes out of your arse, you old bitch.*

CHAPTER NINE

I'm *this* close to using my weapon on the wall. Doing something to get this anger out of me. Beryl's had a bloody heart attack. How inconsiderate is *that*? I won't be able to witness the fruits of my labours now, see her pain and sorrow.

I think of Alfie and how we used to go out for lunch a couple of times a week once we'd retired. Can't do that now, which is why I meet Beryl. Gets me out of the house.

I've pretended for so long, just like Alfie asked me to, that I've forgotten what it was like back then when I loved Beryl and our other two friends as though they were my sisters.

Thinking about that sends me down memory lane. I hate that lane, with its twists and turns shortly after the Rumours started. The path had been straight up until then, and I'd foolishly thought it would continue that way, mine and Alfie's lives mapped out: house, children, happy together until old age.

Alfie had put paid to that, as had Beryl.

Among others.

How can anyone get over that kind of deception?

I'm hoping my plan helps me get over it, otherwise I'm destined to grow sourer with every passing day.

* * *

"When's the bleedin' train due?" Alfie grumbles — as usual.

I thought I was bitter, but blimey, he's a champion complainer.

"Two minutes according to the board up there." I point — I have to do that. Blind as a bat, he is, or getting there anyway. "See it?" I hold back a laugh, because no, he probably can't see it.

"You'll never get to Heaven," he says.

"That's a shame. I've been in Hell for years and could do with a break."

"Don't start that again." He tugs his coat closed, struggling to do the buttons up with arthritic fingers.

Buggered if I'm helping him.

"Why not?" I ask. "After what I've done for you, I'm entitled to say what I like." How can he not see that? Why does he think it can all be forgotten, his antics, their antics, and I'll just roll over like a dog, waiting for a tummy rub? "I told you a long time ago, the days of me not saying what's on my mind are over."

"You don't completely speak your mind, though, do you," he mumbles.

He might have said it under his breath, but I heard him loud and clear. He has the cheek to pick at me when . . .

"You're nothing but a selfish, nasty bastard," I tell him.

"I've heard it all before, and I'm tired of listening," he says.

"You're tired? Really now. Once you did what you did, you left the rest to me. I'm more tired because of what you asked me to do. Years I put up with it, and look at the thanks I get. And what did you mean about me not completely speaking my mind?"

"If you did, you'd have confronted them, said something again after you made a fool of yourself in the pub that time. Pushed for answers."

I don't have to ask who he's talking about. They've been the bane of my life for donkey's years. "Oh, don't you worry, they'll know soon enough that I'm aware of what they did, and I won't have to say a damn word."

He looks at me, eyes rheumy. I could poke them out if I had a mind.

I do, but I won't.

"What do you mean?" His eyebrows meet in the middle.

"You won't have to worry yourself about it." I glance around the platform, once again checking for that new-fangled CCTV that seems to be everywhere. Only one camera, and it's pointing towards the station door.

"That doesn't sound too good." He sniffs.

There's the rumble of the train, but it isn't the one Alfie thinks we're getting on. It's the one before that, which usually flies straight past. Here it comes, streaking along, the front reminding me of a pointed nose, nothing like the trains in my day.

"Ah, it's here," Alfie says, stepping forward, closer to the platform edge.

"Yes, it's here. My salvation."

"What?"

A quick nudge brings me happiness, Alfie sailing forward, the train smacking into him so fast he disappears. I shriek the shriek of a distraught wife, but inside I'm smiling, knowing the one who made me this revolting, cruel, odious old biddy is no more.

He's gone.

So now I move on to the others. Three down so far, three more to go.

CHAPTER TEN

Tracy finally got around to collecting the names and addresses of family and people associated with Colin Spinks. There were no relatives other than his mother, and Natasha Moss only had her mother, father, and a sister. Still, they'd need to be interviewed just the same. She actioned Nada and Erica to do that together as Tim was still out in Starling Road, waiting for people to return home after work. Lara was to remain behind to continue searching CCTV for anyone suspicious hanging around the pertinent streets between six-thirty and eight.

"I'll go with Damon to Colin's workplace," she said to the women. "There's still a couple of hours left in the day, so we may as well make use of it."

She left the incident room, jerking her head at Damon, and he followed her to her office. With the door closed, she said, "I need to pop in and see Winter. No news of Kane doesn't bode well, does it?"

"No. Maybe you should get Nada to contact him now." Damon rubbed his stomach where he'd been stabbed months ago. "But then again, that might make it look obvious. Like we're using her to see where he is and what he's up to."

"Does it matter?" She cocked her head, raised her eyebrows.

"Well, yeah. He might not tell her anything."

"I see your point. I can't imagine why he'd still be at the crime scene. Colin's body has probably been taken away by now, so what else is there to hang around for? Unless Kane's investigating by himself and plans to turn up here later at the end of the shift."

"God knows. He'll have a shock when he gets here, being off the squad and whatnot."

"Hmm. Shouldn't have been such an arsehole then, should he."

"Trace . . ."

"What? It's true, isn't it? You fuck up, you pay the consequences. Isn't that how it works? Like me forgetting to visit Mrs Spinks. I raced to fix the mistake. I didn't piss off and hide somewhere, stropping about it."

"True."

"You *know* me, Damon. I don't give wankers the time of day. If he's that miffed about not running this squad, you'd think he'd have been sensible and gone to Winter. But no, he goes directly to *my* crime scene and stares me down while he's at it. Not good behaviour if you want to get on in this life."

Damon sighed.

"I'm telling you, there's something else up with that bloke," she said. "Unfortunately — or in my case, fortunately — I haven't got the time to go chasing after him to see what it is. Anyway, back in a minute."

She left, striding through the main room then down the corridor to Winter's office. His door stood open, and he sat at his desk, head bent, a stack of paperwork in front of him.

He glanced up. "Ah. Hello, you. Coming to remind me to send you the coffee link?"

She laughed and entered, closing the door to. She remained in front of it. "No, sir. Any news on Kane?"

"Now here's the thing. I checked with those officers at the crime scene — Newson and the like — and apparently Kane left shortly after you did, mumbling something about it being too close to home." He rubbed his chin. "The only thing I can imagine that relates to is the case that did a number on him. I assume the murder victim today was in a bit of a state, was it?"

"Yes, sir. Head smashed in."

"Hmm. The victims in that case of his were a sight, too, so maybe it's that. I didn't realise it had affected him *that* much. Damn man doesn't really open up. All the more reason for him to take some leave, get some counselling."

So that the conversation didn't turn to *her* getting counselling, she said, "Before I go out to chat to Colin's work colleagues, I'll ask Nada to get in contact with Kane and I'll let you know the outcome. I'll text you, if that's all right, sir, as I need to be getting on."

"Fine by me. I'll give him a bell myself. In fact, I'll do it now. Wait there a second."

The call produced nothing except the ringing of the connection, it seemed, so Winter texted him.

"If he doesn't answer me," he said, "I'm going to have to go down a road I don't want to go, but that's not your problem."

"Sorry about this, sir. I have to go. I'll let you know if anything significant crops up." She opened the door.

"You do that. Good luck."

"Thanks."

She went straight to Nada, who was just about to leave with Erica. Pulling Nada to one side, she said, "Can you do as you suggested and try getting hold of Kane, see what the hell's up with him, please?"

"Will do." Nada smiled. "Now?"

"Give it until after you've been to see Natasha Moss' family — actually, leave her and her mother alone for now, I'll deal with them in the morning. Just see the father and sister."

"Yes, boss. Anything else you want us to do?"

"No. Your interviews will already take you past the end of the shift, and as we have no other lines to follow, you two may as well head off home after. I will, however, be getting hold of you if I need you to come back in before the morning. Sorry about that, but murder is more important than sleep in my book."

"It's fine," Nada said.

"Look, what do you know about Kane's state of mind from that big case you had a while back? This time last year — the bonfire murder. That one. I've had information that he got involved with a woman."

"Um . . ." Nada shifted from foot to foot. "This feels rotten talking about him like this, to be honest."

"I realise that, Nada, but I'm concerned he isn't coping well, and him behaving like he has since I came on the scene might have triggered something. I won't go into details, but I know damn well how straw can break a camel's back, and one little thing can bring everything rushing at you and it sets you off. If him going AWOL today is something to do with that case, tell me. He's been an utter arsehole, yes, but we were friends once — more than that, as I said earlier — and I don't want him losing his career if we can help him. See? I'm not a bitch really, just that I'm frustrated he's done this when we have a murder on our hands."

"Err, there were rumours he got a bit attached to a woman called Charlotte Rothers. Jez Pickins' girlfriend — the drug dealer Kane was after. Kane had been tracking Pickins for months. He'd met Charlotte accidentally on purpose to see if she'd give him information on Pickins. Kane and Charlotte ended up . . . well, you know, and then everything else happened. In the end, they didn't continue their relationship, but I think he wanted to. That's about all I know on that score. He was pissed off for a while, then after the trial and Henry Cobbings had been sentenced, he seemed even more pissed off." Nada sighed. "I asked him what was wrong, and he said he'd gone round to see Charlotte, see if she was all right after the verdict, and she'd gone. Skipped town. He tried finding her — on the quiet, like — but so far, nothing."

Cogs clicked in Tracy's mind. What if Kane felt incompetent with her around? What if him failing to find Charlotte upset him, then Tracy coming along had confirmed he wasn't good enough for the job let alone tracking an ex-lover?

"Thanks, Nada, that helps a lot. Right, I'd best be going."

"See you, boss." Nada met Erica at the door, and the pair left.

Tracy scratched her head. "Lara, you all right to man the phones as well as watching the CCTV until I get back?"

Lara sniffed. Clearly a team member who might take a while to come around to the new way of things. "Yes, boss." Sullen. Spoilt brat syndrome.

Tracy couldn't be doing with it. "If you have something you need to get off your chest, best you do it now. I *really* don't put up with crap, Lara." *Not since before I was eighteen and left home.*

Lara flushed and turned in her chair to face Tracy. "I . . . I don't think it's appropriate that I say anything . . ." She glanced at Damon, who sat on Nada's desk.

"What, with Damon here?" Tracy asked.

Lara nodded.

"Easily sorted." Tracy looked at him. "My office, please."

He poked his tongue out — *you little sod* — and went on his way.

"Right, out with it." *Like she's going to want to open up with the way you bark at people.* "Sorry." She cleared her throat. "Okay. What's wrong?" Softer tone. Another new Tracy. What was one more persona on top of all the others from the Past, eh?

Lara's already red cheeks flared brighter. "Oh God, this is so awkward. I'm sodding conflicted. Sorry for swearing."

"I don't give a shit about swearing. See? I said shit. It's a word. Who cares. Go on. This won't go any further if I can help it. That make you feel better?"

Lara nodded. "I've . . . um . . . me and Kane . . ."

"Ah. I see. *Now* I understand your attitude towards me."

"I'm so sorry. I don't usually go against orders, but he's . . ."

"You like him a lot."

"Yes."

"So what the hell's the deal with him today, do you know?"

Lara shrugged. "He's been off lately — at work and with me. Like he doesn't want to be with me. I told him if he wanted to end it to just say so, but he said he had things on his mind." She bit her lip. "Then yesterday . . . This is going to sound bad, and I'm not a snoop, okay? But he left a notebook at my place. Um . . ."

"You looked inside, yes?"

She blew air out. "I did. I hate myself for it."

"So what did you find?"

"Stuff about that Charlotte woman. Train times. He'd written Cornwall down. So I texted him, said his book was at mine, and he . . . he shot round really quick, snatched it off my table, said, 'Did you read it?' I lied and said no, but he knew. I could tell by his face."

"Then what?"

"He said, 'I'm going to find her, you know that, don't you?' And I shrugged — I mean, what could I say to that? He left, didn't speak to me this morning when I turned up for work — not one-on-one, anyway — and I took it that we're done, finished. He's still got feelings for her."

"I'm sorry you're going through this," Tracy said. "But him treating you like that, plus how he's been today . . . Not good, is it? He's hardly reliable material, if you catch my drift. Maybe you're better off with someone else. Between you and me, back in the day he slept around, then after we finished, he said he was giving relationships a wide berth. Maybe when he met Charlotte something clicked, and he hasn't got over it. Maybe being with you . . ."

"He was seeing if he was over her. Using me. Yes, I got that impression anyway, but stupid me, I thought I could make him forget her." She swiped a tear off her cheek. "Men are bastards."

"I used to think that." *God, did I believe that.* "But not all of them are. Take a break from them then dive back in. Someone will come along, you'll see."

Tracy rested a hand on Lara's shoulder. Lara smiled, a sad one, then straightened her spine.

"D'you know what, you're all right, boss."

Tracy laughed. "Told you I wasn't so bad. Okay, I'm off." She moved to the exit. "Damon! We need to go."

He came; they went.

CHAPTER ELEVEN

On the journey to Colin Spinks' place of work, Tracy told Damon what Nada and Lara had said.

"Fucking hell, sounds like he's got it bad for this Charlotte then," he said.

"Must have if he's done what I suspect. After all this time, too. It's been a good year since he first met her. Do you think he's actually gone down to Cornwall — if that's even where she is?"

Damon shrugged. "Might have. I know if it were me, and you'd left town . . ."

What have I done to deserve him? She had no idea. "Same the other way around." She gave his thigh a quick pat. *Swiftly getting off this topic* . . . "Wouldn't it have been better to tell Winter he needed an immediate break, though?"

"Probably. Maybe he's just decided to make himself scarce for today and he'll be back tomorrow — not that he'll be working with us, but you know what I mean."

"Here we are, look." Tracy pulled up outside a shop — SPINKS' CLEANING SERVICES — situated beside a Costa.

The obvious hit her. Colin had owned the place — or was it his mum's? This opened up a whole new set of questions. Did he owe money to creditors? Was there a disgruntled customer out there? Had he pissed off an employee?

"Hmm," Damon said.

"My thoughts exactly," Tracy said. "Off we go then."

They left the car and entered the shop, Tracy approaching the counter where a forty-something bloke stood behind it pinning labels on clear plastic covers protecting shirts and jackets that had presumably been dry cleaned. He turned and smiled, abandoning his job to come closer to the till.

The shoulder-length, straggly dark mop on his head needed a good wash. "Here to pick something up?" he asked, the smile that followed bright.

Nice teeth, shame about the exceptionally long, wiry black hair growing out of a large mole on his cheek. His eyes were all right, too, if you liked insipid blue with red veins streaking over the whites.

Such a judgmental bitch, Tracy.

I know. Can't seem to stop myself.

"Only information." Tracy smiled back. "DI Collier, and this is DS Hanks." She showed him her ID.

He paled, took a step back. Pressed one hand to his chest. Had he been in trouble with the law before or what?

"Nothing for you to worry about, sir." Tracy rested her hands on the counter and wrinkled her nose. The cleaning products used here were strongly scented. "Have you heard the news?"

"News?" He frowned. Rubbed his cheek, his alarming mole hair sticking out between two fingers. "Well, I saw a bit on breakfast TV before work, something about a hurricane. Oh, and someone getting stabbed in London. That what you mean?"

Tracy's turn to frown. Hadn't Natasha Moss phoned to let this man know, or had she been too distraught to even think about the shop?

Would you think about the shop if it were Damon?

No. Absolutely no.

Well then.

"Um, no," Tracy said. "Not that kind of news. What's your name, sir?" Her eyes watered from a massive cloud of steam coming out from a doorway to the rear of the shop. "Um, something going on back there you need to see to?"

He glanced behind him. "No, it's just the steamer. Lou's out there doing a wedding dress. A woman wants to sell it a year after she got married. He left her. Went off with some other bird."

Sad, but blimey, she didn't need gossip — unless it helped the case.

"Your name?" she prompted.

"Oh, Wesley — Wes Farthing, like the bike, only I haven't got two wheels, I've got legs, but I do have a penny." He grinned and laughed — more like a wheeze really. Muttley.

Tracy supposed she was meant to find that funny. She didn't. "Right, Mr Farthing. Are you a manager here?"

"Only today and Saturdays when Colin — Mr Spinks, my boss — has his days off. Other days I'm just a regular employee."

"Does that bother you, being a *regular* employee?" She raised her eyebrows.

"Nope. Prefer it, to be fair. Less worry, know what I mean? Like, today and Saturdays I have to sort the takings, make sure they're locked in the safe. I've got to think about people coming in and robbing the place — been robbed twice before, see, and I was here both times. Shit the life out of me when they brought out a sodding knife. It's getting bad round here, but you'd know that anyway, wouldn't you?"

"I agree, Mr Farthing. Very bad." She paused for a moment to make him sweat, staring him right in the eye. "Does every employee get along with Mr Spinks?"

"As far as I know," he said.

"Do *you* like Mr Spinks?"

He jerked his head back, creating two extra chins. "Of course I bloody do. Known him for years. Gave me a job when I got out of the nick, he did, when no one else would."

Tracy's interest piqued. "What were you inside for?"

"Didn't pay my council tax. It pissed me off, because I explained I was skint, on hard times, but they wouldn't listen. I'd only missed six months and all." He shook his head. "I wouldn't mind if they used it to fix the pot holes in the roads or made sure the kiddie park was safe and free of broken glass from those teenagers chucking beer bottles down. But they don't, do they? God knows what they spend it on, but it isn't on anything I can see."

Satisfied he wasn't someone she needed to worry too much about, Tracy asked, "Are you able to manage this shop for a longer period of time, do you think?"

"I could. I wouldn't want to. As I said, the responsibility . . . Err, why?"

"I'm sure Miss Moss will be contacting you shortly, but I'm afraid there's some unfortunate news I have to share with you. First, though, do you know of anyone who was upset with Mr Spinks?"

"Unfortunate news?" His mouth dropped open, and his eyes bugged out, the light blue turning darker.

"Answer my question first, Mr Farthing."

"Anyone upset with Colin?" He blinked rapidly. "No one would be. He's a top bloke, he is. Help anyone out. Has something happened?"

"One more question, if I may. Do you know if this place is leased or mortgaged?"

"Leased, and I only know that because we get rental inspectors nosing about every six months. Their visits usually fall on Colin's days off, and I have to deal with them. They check the building then leave."

"Do you know who owns it?"

"Yeah, Genie Rentals, that gaff down Loomings Street. D'you know the one? Owner is a Mr Vellum. Old boy, about sixty-five, knew Colin's dad back in the day, when this shop was run by him."

Tracy glanced at Damon to make sure he was writing that down. "Thank you, Mr Farthing. Unfortunately, the news isn't good." *Here we go, Tracy Blunt Collier.* "Mr Spinks has died."

"What?" He flapped a hand in front of his face, his hair wafting in the breeze.

Don't look too closely or you'll see his mole hair waving.

Tracy!

"Are you all right, Mr Farthing?" Damon asked, stepping in with the empathy Tracy rarely seemed able to muster. "You're a bit white. Have a seat, will you?"

Damon moved around the counter, dragged an orange plastic chair closer to Mr Farthing, and took off the stack of small boxes on top of it, placing them on the floor. Mr Farthing sat, his cheeks now glowing red, his bottom lip wet and wobbling.

"That's . . . that's a bit of a shock," he said.

"It usually is, Mr Farthing, and I'm sorry I had to bring such upsetting news." *There you go, I* can *be kind.* "Do you want me to tell . . . Lou, is it? The man out the back?"

"Woman," he said, staring vacantly into the middle distance. "Louise Vale. Old dear who helps out twice a week with the big stuff. Wedding dresses, like I said. Duvets and whatnot. It's best I tell her."

Another billow of steam chuntered out from the back, indicating Lou Vale was still at work, none the wiser.

Shame she couldn't stay that way.

"All right," Tracy said. "I'll leave that to you then. Do you need a cup of tea? I can nip to Costa, if you like?"

Mr Farthing nodded, looking as though he wasn't the quickest bunny in the forest, and Tracy sighed with relief that he wanted a drink. She could do with a coffee — and a breather from the man's distress. Tears tumbled down his cheeks, and he sniffed.

"Won't be long," she said, leaving Damon behind the counter with him, pushing out into the clearer air that wasn't riddled with the stench of chemicals.

The five or so minutes she spent in Costa gave her a moment to think and, armed with a cup-holder tray containing a coffee each for herself and Damon, and teas for Farthing and Vale, she returned to the dry cleaners.

Farthing stood, leaning his hands on the counter, head bent, still off with the fairies, the poor sod. Damon waited on the customer side, hands clasped behind his back. She smiled at him to show her appreciation that he'd watched over Farthing while she'd been gone, and he returned it and shrugged as if to say: *I don't know how to deal with him like that.*

Tracy set the tray on the counter and decided on being brisk to snap Farthing out of his trance. "Right, then. Here you go. There's one for Lou as well." She lifted Farthing's tea and held it out to him.

He raised his head and stared at her — or was that through her? — with watery eyes. "Um, thank you."

"Get that down you. It'll help," she said. "Sit on that chair again."

He did, then sipped his drink.

"Perhaps you ought to close the shop for the day, hmm?" she asked. "It's almost closing time anyway. A few minutes early won't hurt." Taking matters into her own hands, she flipped the sign over on the door and clicked the lock. "There. That'll save you worrying someone's going to come in, won't it. And if they knock on the door, that's tough. You have more to think about than them."

He nodded. "I feel so bad, but . . ."

"What's the matter?" Tracy asked, a bit snappish. She hadn't meant it to come out like that.

"What will I do for a job now if this place gets shut down?" He closed his eyes for a second or two. "I shouldn't even be thinking that. There's poor Natasha on her own now, and there's Colin's mum, Beryl, and here I am, worrying about my job, about *me*."

"That's natural, Mr Farthing." Tracy passed Damon his coffee. "Life goes on. Just because Mr Spinks has died, doesn't mean your life stops as well, does it. But I imagine Miss Moss will want to keep the shop going, won't she?" Here was a chance to find out if Colin was killed so the business could be sold and Natasha would benefit.

"Yes, she'd keep it going. She used to work here before she had the baby. That's how they met. Knows what she's doing here, she does." Farthing smiled sadly. "Such a shame. They were getting married soon."

Heartless as it may seem, Tracy didn't fancy being an emotional prop any longer. "There you go, then. You won't need to find another job, will you."

"How . . ." Farthing cleared his throat. "How did Colin die?"

Ah. Tracy had been waiting for that. If he hadn't asked, she would have suspected him of already knowing. Then again, some killers were smart and asked anyway.

"We're not at liberty to say at the moment," she said. *Liar. You just don't want to deal with the fallout.* "Perhaps speak to Miss Moss. Give her a day or two, though, all right?"

He nodded. "I'll open up each day in the meantime."

"You do that. Okay, we'll be going now." She plucked a card out of her pocket and tossed it on the counter. "Give me a bell if you think of anything that might help. Um . . . if you hear of anyone who had a problem with Mr Spinks."

He dipped his head.

With nothing further to say, Tracy took her coffee and led the way out of the shop. On the street, she sighed again and got into the car. Damon followed, and they sat sipping for a while, Tracy staring through the windscreen.

"I need to look up the Vale woman's phone number when we get back to the station. I'll speak to her on the blower, seeing as she's an old lady. If she's anything like Hilda Jones, I don't want to speak to her face to face."

"I wouldn't either," Damon said.

Silence reigned, Damon drumming his fingertips on one knee.

"What are you thinking?" she asked.

"About what?"

"About this case."

"Hmm. It seems like a random attack to me."

"Why randomly attack someone for no reason, though? He wasn't robbed. All he was doing was walking home with a bag of sodding Pampers. Hardly seems right he was walloped on the head for that, does it. I mean, there has to be some other motive."

"Unless there isn't one, and someone out there just fancied killing. It happens. You know the specs on serial killers. They think about it for years then do it. Might not even know the victim, they just choose them because they happen to be there at the right time."

"But this isn't a serial killer. It's a one-off, got to be." She finished her coffee and stuffed the cup into the compartment in her door. The top pinged off and landed by her foot.

"At the moment." Damon glanced at her, rubbing his forehead.

"Don't say that."

"Say what?"

"That we have another serial to deal with. Like . . . like *back then*."

He reached over and stroked her cheek with the backs of his fingers. "It's going to come up again at some point, Trace." He lowered his hand to rest it on her thigh. "Serials aren't going to stop happening just because you dealt with one in the past and it involved your family, and you don't want a repeat. And we just have to hope *that* killer isn't going to do it again, don't we. Because this squad covers *that* city, so we're going to end up working that patch again one day." He paused. "So we haven't really got a fresh start."

"I know . . ." *She's out there, my damn sister, and she could be doing this all over again.* It couldn't be Lisa, could it? She'd been forced into committing murder last time. Tracy doubted she'd *choose* to do it now.

"And if we *do* end up having to deal with a serial, then we deal with it," he said. "That's why we agreed to move here so you could head the squad, to stop people like *her*."

"Among other things." She pinched her bottom lip.

"Yes, among other things. It was time to get out of that city, away from the memories. Not just for you, but for me, too. I had to leave to stop the reminders of being stabbed bugging me. To stop the thoughts of bumping into the woman who did it and worrying whether she'll decide to come back for another go."

"She wouldn't." *I hope.* "Surely she wouldn't be stupid enough to come back."

"You never know, do you? She needs help in dealing with the trauma she went through. Living out in the real world after doing what she did could—"

"Stop it. I don't want to talk about it. Look, she got away, okay? That's the end of it." *I can't talk about it in case I slip up and tell you I let her walk free.* She threw out her tumultuous thoughts like so much bad rubbish. "Anyway, we agreed to start again with a clean slate and not discuss her. Or *him.*" *My father will haunt me until the day I join him in Hell, so not talking about him won't make a blind bit of difference. He's still there, inside me, laughing with his ghost laugh, tormenting me.* "So, we deal with this case as though it could be anyone, same as we would if *he* hadn't . . . Enough. Let's forget about it. About those two."

She started the engine and nudged the car out onto the road. Damon didn't speak on the journey to the station, and when they arrived, he went off to the loo.

She walked into the incident room to find it empty.

Apart from Kane sitting at Nada's desk, using her computer.

Oh shit.

CHAPTER TWELVE

"Um, what are you doing here?" Tracy asked.

Kane jumped and closed the window on the monitor. Clearly, he'd been engrossed in whatever he was doing and hadn't heard her enter.

"I work here," he said.

Tracy snorted. "Could have fooled me. Not seen much work out of you so far. Unless you count work as prowling around the crime scene this morning. Where have you been all day since then?" She walked to Nada's desk and folded her arms, purposely encroaching on his personal space.

"None of your business," he snapped.

"I think you'll find it is, Kane." She sat on the edge, her thigh almost touching the side of the keyboard.

He leant back in the chair and stared up at her. "Look, I fucked up today, all right? Something . . . something came up, and I had to do—"

"Do what? Do some investigating on the side trying to find Charlotte Rothers?"

His face paled. "How . . . ?"

"I'm a fucking detective, Kane." Tracy sighed. "So, you did whatever it was you did, and went wherever it was you went because . . . ?"

"I have a feeling she's up to something," he admitted.

"Okay, and that means you can eff off willy-nilly, does it, when we have a *murder* case to deal with? I understand you being narked about me heading this squad, but that isn't my fault. A position came up; I took it, simple as. I have my reasons for coming here, for leaving the city, and to get here and find one of the best detectives I know swanning off on the job . . . Not great, is it. And considering your old partner did the same to you . . ." She raised her eyebrows. "See what I'm getting at? Pot, kettle, anyone?"

He nodded, cheeks flushing. "I'm sorry. I mean that. I'm . . . she got to me, okay? I really liked her. Still do. Charlotte was different. Broken and . . ."

"You wanted to fix her, but she fucked off to fix herself, yes? She didn't need DI Barnett, and that's got to burn."

"Yes." He massaged his temples. "Then you turned up this morning and . . . What a bloody mess."

"Yep. Especially because you're no longer on the squad."

"What?" He dropped his hands to the armrests and gripped them tight, knuckles white and bony, stretching the skin.

"Winter made the decision after I told him you'd gone AWOL. Don't look at me like that. I'm entitled to report people on my team if they're not up to scratch. I've got Erica with us in your place — not that she's as good as you. I could have done with you on my side, but you decided to bugger off on a case of your own making, so . . ."

"Shit." He let his head fall back against the seat.

"Did you think you could just do that and nothing would happen?" she asked.

"Um . . . yes?"

She grunted. "Maybe when you were in charge, but not now. Kane, you know I don't suffer fools gladly, and with such a big case to deal with, I can't carry dead wood. You're that wood. Still, there's always a bright side. You've got enforced leave — no idea how long — so you can go off and find Charlotte without letting anyone down."

"Are you *serious*?"

"Is this face smiling? Yes, I'm fucking serious. You'd best go and see Winter. The sooner you do that, the sooner you can find her, can't you." She pushed off the desk and walked towards the door leading to the hallway. "Oh, and rumours. You know how people talk. It would be nice if you let Lara know where she stands, wouldn't it? You're not an arsehole, Kane, so don't start acting like one now."

She stepped inside her office, emotionally wired, and closed the door. She hoped that twazzock in the incident room found that woman — and the relationship he so obviously wanted with her. With no desire to think about him any longer, she sat at her desk and booted up her computer. Finding the telephone number for Louise Vale, she scribbled it on a pad then made the call, hoping the woman would be home by now.

"Yes?" a woman answered.

"Ah, Mrs Vale? My name is—"

"You're assuming I'm a Mrs, then?"

Is this going to be Hilda Jones all over again? Christ, give me a damn break.

"I apologise, *Ms* Vale. I'm Detective Inspector Tracy Collier, and I'm calling about your boss, Mr Spinks."

"What about him?"

Wow. "Did Mr Farthing tell you the news?"

"What news?"

Oh, for fuck's sake.

"About Mr Spinks." Tracy bit her bottom lip. Hard.

"Oh, *that* news. Yes. He told me the sort of questions you asked, and I'm afraid I'm no good to you. I don't have any information for you."

"Oh. Right." *Well, that was short and sweet.* "When did you start working at the dry cleaners?"

"A couple of years ago now. Colin needed some help. I only do one day a week — his mum, Beryl, comes in, too. Then there's Hilda—"

Hilda? Is she fucking kidding me?

"Hilda who?" Tracy asked, then held her breath.

"Jones," Ms Vale said.

Oh, dear Lord . . .

"Okay, thank you. How often does Hilda work at the cleaners?"

"Once a week. She does the same as me. The quilts and heavy things that need steaming, although she's not as adept at it as me. I'm a viable employee — she isn't. She calls in sick sometimes, whereas *I* turn up whether my body's giving me gyp or not."

"Well, thank you for that information, Ms Vale, I appreciate it. I'll let you go now and—"

"Good. I haven't got time for gossiping. I need to get the dinner on."

Taken aback by the woman's abruptness, Tracy said goodbye and ended the call.

Dinner. That sounded good.

She returned to the incident room. Kane had gone. She added more information to the whiteboard then checked Erica's notepad for any jottings about Spinks. Seemed Erica had found some old friends of his from school and college. She'd ticked off who she'd called and had written details of the conversations beside each name. No one appeared to have spoken to Spinks in years except on Facebook.

Beside the notepad, a printout on white A4 had Spinks' Facebook friends on it, their ages, and what they did for a living. Tracy assumed these people had listed such things on their profiles. He only had thirty-four friends, but some of them were business associates from what she could gather. People who sold cleaning products, folks like that. So it seemed he'd led quite the solitary life in terms of social interaction, probably preferring to stay at home with Natasha and the baby.

So why the hell had someone wanted to kill him?

Was Damon right after all and this was a random attack?

Damon waltzed in.

"Took your time in the loo," she said, going back to the board and pinning up the A4 with Blu Tack.

"I heard you and Kane talking. Thought it best I steer clear."

"Good thinking. Get yourself up to speed on this." She prodded a finger at the printout. "I need a wee myself."

She left the room, heading down the corridor where Winter's office was. Voices — Winter's and Kane's — floated through the door, and she hesitated. Eavesdroppers never heard anything good about themselves, but she didn't give much of a shit if she heard them talking about her. Did she?

"You were out of order." Winter.

"I'm sorry, sir, but I don't think that case is finished."

"What do you mean?"

"She . . . Look, I can't go into details because . . . well, I just can't, but I'm telling you, she still has a bone to pick with Henry Cobbings. He's in Devon, doing his stretch for murder, and I heard she's moved to Cornwall."

"And? Maybe she fancied the seaside life. Lots of people do. Who did you hear that from?"

"Her mother — who, by the way, says she has no idea specifically where Charlotte has gone except she knows it's Cornwall."

"Do you believe her?"

"Yes."

"And instead of me signing you off on leave, you expect me to allow you to go poking around in Cornwall, paid to do it, based on some hunch, and pissing off the coppers there?"

"Well, I wouldn't put it quite like that."

"I would. And the answer is no."

"But, sir . . ."

"No, Kane. Absolutely not. You were needed here, and you messed that up. Now you can face the consequences. I want you to see a counsellor weekly, and you're not to come back here until a month from today. Now, that's the end of it. No more arguing. And if you feel you can't work with Tracy . . ."

Tracy buggered off before she heard any more. She visited the toilet then dashed past Winter's office and into the incident room. Damon sat at Erica's desk, reading the notepad.

"Time to call it a day," she said. "I'm tired, and we've got nothing much to go on until any fingerprints come back off that receipt and the Asda sticker. And you just know there are going to be loads of them. We'll pick this up again in the morning."

She switched off the lights, and they made their way down to the car. She drove through town, and a Chinese takeaway had her stomach rumbling, so she pulled over.

"I can't be arsed to cook. Want the same as you usually have?" She gestured to the yellow sign with red writing: CHINA KITCHEN.

"Please. I'll wait in here."

She frowned. "You okay?"

"Just a bit sore sometimes." He patted his stomach. The stabbed area.

"Sore how?" She rested a hand on his shoulder, worry chewing on her innards with blunt teeth.

"The scar tissue, I assume. Goes all tight. Pulls. Aches."

She should have arrested her sister and made her pay just for knifing Damon, but oddly, she understood why Lisa had done it. Tracy didn't condone it, but . . . "I'm so sorry that happened. If you weren't involved with me—"

"No, it would have happened anyway. We're partners at work. She'd have gone for me just for that. She picked someone you cared about. It's not your fault your dad and that woman . . . Sorry. I'll shut up."

"Thank you. So, dinner, wine, sleep."

"Sounds good to me."

She entered the takeaway, greeted by the smell every Chinese seemed to have. After ordering more food than they could eat, she clutched the white token she'd been given with a black number five on it and stared out of the floor-to-ceiling window at the dark street. People either strode in eagerness to get home or sluggishly plodded along, weary from the day. An off-license opposite had an offer on, a big neon-orange poster in the window, three bottles of wine for the price of one, and it still worked out more expensive than the equivalent from the supermarket. She'd nip to Asda after this, pick up a red and a white.

A woman came in, long black hair, navy-blue coat with the hood up. She had her head down, but she peered at Tracy sideways, eyes thin slits. Tracy's stomach roiled. The woman looked like her mother would with dark hair, the same face as the EFIT from the case involving her father and sister . . .

Fuck no. Tell me that isn't her.

Tracy took two steps towards her.

Oh God, no. No . . .

"Lisa?" she hissed, going right up to her and grabbing her arm to guide her into the corner beside the door. "What the *hell*?"

"I needed to see you. I'm not doing so well," Lisa said.

Now Tracy had a good look at her, she could determine that for herself. Dark shadows beneath the eyes, hair unwashed, hanging in stringy noodles. Pasty skin, possibly from lack of good food, bad health, hollows above prominent, pointy cheekbones.

"You weren't supposed to stay around here," Tracy whispered, glancing out through the window to see if Damon had clocked them. "You were meant to have disappeared."

"I know. I did for a bit, but . . . I've got a cash-in-hand job, a bedsit provided by my boss, but *it* won't go away."

It.

The Past.

No, it never went away. It kept popping up in Tracy's face — like now.

"I went to the station in the city to find you, and they said you'd moved here," Lisa said, wringing her hands, nails bitten to ragged stumps, the cuticles red, inflamed. "I have no one else to turn to."

Don't play that card, Lisa.

"So how did you get that information?" Tracy gritted her teeth. "Did you just walk into the bloody station when there was an EFIT of you on the board in the foyer last time I was there? Because that's a sodding brilliant thing to do, isn't it, getting yourself recognised."

Lisa's teeth chattered. "I phoned. Told whoever it was I spoke to — might have been a man called Mark — that I needed to talk to you urgently about a case."

Mark. One of the men in her old team.

She didn't need Lisa here, fucking everything up. If Damon found out she hadn't trusted him with what she'd done . . . If Winter found out . . .

"Did Mark ask what you wanted?"

"Yes, but I put the phone down."

"Listen, You can't be here," Tracy said. "We can't be seen together, you know that, for your safety as well as my career. Do you *know* how much shit I'd be in if my new boss found out I'd seen you and didn't arrest you?" She lowered her voice. "They have no idea what your name is — they think you were *his* girlfriend and believe you got away. It needs to stay like that. If you hang around here — if Damon sees you, for fuck's sake — he'll arrest you without a second thought for stabbing him. They'll question you — they think *you* killed those people."

"I didn't kill all of them." She scowled.

"I know you didn't, but because *he* killed the ones you didn't . . . They might think you were in on it together. I let you go because you didn't deserve to switch the prison of home for another one, do you understand? Don't mess this up." She looked through the window again at her car, just making Damon out with his head back, probably shutting his eyes for a bit. "How did you find me here?"

"Followed you all day from the police station."

"You have a car?"

"Yes."

"Where are you living?"

"Here."

"Oh, for God's sake, Lisa!"

"Number Five," the bloke behind the counter called.

Tracy pointed at Lisa to stay put and collected her box of food. She pushed Lisa onto the bench seat in front of the window, placing the box beside her. "Wait there a minute. Do *not* go anywhere."

Out on the street, Tracy scanned the buildings for a bank then ran down the pavement to a Lloyds. She withdrew two hundred and fifty pounds off her credit card. Back in the Chinese — thank God Lisa was still there — she asked the man behind the counter for a carrier bag. He handed her a white one, and she placed two of the cartons inside it, the contents written on the lids. Box under one arm, she stared down at Lisa, who gazed up, so pitiful, eyes just like their mother's it hurt to look at them.

"Here." Tracy handed her the bag of food. "And take this as well." The money. "I feel awful, but we can't see each other again. It's for your own good." *And mine. So much for mine. Please don't fuck my life up, Lisa. Not now* he's *gone and everything's working out. I deserve peace as much as you do.*

"Thanks." Lisa pouted. "This is harder than I thought it would be."

"I know. I can imagine."

"Can you? Can you *really*?"

No. If she were honest, she couldn't. Imagining being locked up in a basement and abused by their father for most of her life . . . No, she couldn't comprehend that. It was bad enough Tracy had endured the same *without* being held prisoner in the house. But it was Lisa's cross to bear — Tracy's, too, but she wasn't responsible for what their father had done, and she couldn't — wouldn't — keep paying the price for his warped sins.

"We can't see each other again, understand?" God, she felt a bitch, but it was for the best.

"I understand."

"Go back to your bedsit. Never come near me again. And if you see me in this town or the city — work means I'll be there sometimes — do *not* acknowledge me. And it might be an idea to buy some fake glasses. It's so obvious who you are without any. The dye job on your hair isn't enough."

She walked out then, hating herself but knowing self-preservation was key.

In the car, Damon asked, "I see you nipped to the bank."

Shit. Did he spot me talking to Lisa as well?

"I did. Fancied wine. I'll pop to Asda now."

"Not like you to use cash."

Bloody hell . . .

She shrugged. "Spanish inquisition or what."

"Sorry. Just found it weird, that's all."

"Well don't. For all you know, I could need cash to buy you something."

"Do you?"

"No."

"So . . ."

"Oh, for Pete's sake. I drew cash out. Big deal. Get over it."

She sped away from the kerb.

Up ahead, Lisa shuffled along the pavement, eating noodles using her fingers.

Christ, she must be hungry.

Don't think about her. You did what you could.

Tracy opened her mind box, the one that held all her secrets, and stuffed a new one inside. No one — *no one* — could know she'd just aided a criminal for the second time. Ever.

CHAPTER THIRTEEN

It's dark now, so I'm safe to go out. Sturdy boots on, gloves, calf-length black coat, weapon in hand. About to open the front door, I'm startled by the shape of someone through the mottled glass. It can only be *him*, going by the height and width, and it's getting on my wick him keep calling round.

Why didn't he just fuck off years ago?

I rest my weapon against the wall then take the security chain off and swing the door back. And yes, it's him, standing there like a dippy version of Uncle Fester, only younger and without that weird-shaped nose. I could just clout him right now, around the earhole, give him a piece of my mind about continually invading my privacy.

Pointless, though. It'll fall on deaf ears; it usually does.

"Off out, are you?" he asks, stepping inside, like I even invited him.

What right has he to do that?

"No, I just came back in, actually." I take my coat off, hang it on the wonky hook, playing out the charade. It's for the greater good. "What's it to you anyway? My keeper, are you?"

"Just making conversation."

"Well don't."

I go into the living room, annoyed because I might miss my next target now if *he* stays too long. I'll be nastier than ever; that'll make him leave faster, the prat. In my chair, I stare at the blank TV. He walks in, his reflection on the screen, lurching along to the sofa. He reminds me of someone else, the way he walks, and it sets my teeth on edge. He flops onto the couch and slaps his hands on his thighs.

"What do you want?" I snap. "You know I like watching my soaps of an evening. Having you here puts me off. I can't concentrate on what's going on with you warbling in the background or scrolling through that bleedin' phone of yours."

"Pardon me for coming round to see if you're all right."

"I won't pardon you for anything, you ingrate. You don't deserve a pardon. You shouldn't even exist." I give him a nasty glare. It has my eyes watering. It's got nothing to do with anything else. Nothing at all.

"What's that supposed to mean?"

His mouth flops open, and I want to fill it with my fist. Knock his damn teeth out. *Such* a little bastard. I can't bear the sight of him so turn to the TV again. He's on there, his head, shoulders, and the back of the sofa a silhouette.

I give the wood flooring my attention instead. "Never you mind what it means. So, answer me. What do you want?"

"I just wanted to know if you'll be okay when we move to Scotland. It's been bothering me since I told you."

"Bothering you?" Indignance rises inside me, bitter and sharp, and I whip my head round to gape at him. "It can't bother you that much, otherwise you wouldn't be leaving at all, would you? If you *cared*, you'd stay. If you *cared*, you wouldn't be such an arsehole."

"Yet again, you can't stay civil for even five minutes. I can't hack this." He pushes himself up off the sofa and gives me his variety of my nasty glare.

Cheeky shit.

"Can't hack what?" I stand, hands on hips, checking the time on the wall clock.

Get out. Go back to your scabby wife and kids.

"You," he says. "The way you are. The way you treat me."

"You're like a broken record."

"I'm going home."

"You do that."

He leaves the room, and I follow him.

I remember the spoils I picked up from Colin. "There's a packet of Pampers in the kitchen on the side. For the little one."

He turns in the hallway, frowning so hard his brow is like the sand when we went to Weymouth once, where the sea had gone over it and created smooth ruffles.

"I'll never understand you," he says, dipping into the kitchen to collect the nappies then coming out again, holding them up. "You even got the right size, look. Thank you."

"Yes, well . . . Take them and bugger off. Don't say I never give you anything."

He seems confused. "You're all right every now and again, aren't you."

"If you say so. Now get lost. *Corrie* is on in a minute."

He moves to hug me, or, God forbid, kiss my cheek, but I shoo him away, closing the door behind him. Coat back on, I wait for a few minutes, annoyed because of the interruption. If his visit has ruined my plans, I'll swing for him.

I'm going to swing for him anyway.

Confidence returning, I collect my weapon and leave, going to the left towards the recreation ground a few streets away. The next person in my plan is playing five-a-side football there tonight, some charity game or other, and it'll just about be over by the time I arrive. I'd planned to watch from the tree line, hidden, to stare at him while he kicked the ball about and let my hate fester for an hour or so, but there's no time for that now.

The players walk off the pitch, an Astro Turf effort that's skinned the knees of a couple of the blokes. Big kids, they are, and it seems to me they haven't had the memo about growing up. He's messing around with his boot laces while the others troop into the white, pebble-dash changing room block. There's a red-brick clubhouse next to it, where they'll no doubt go and sink a few beers before going home to their wives. *He* never goes in for a bevvy. He has a wife to get back to. Kids. He's a good man, so his mother continually used to tell me, but that makes no odds to me. He is what he is, and I can't tolerate that any longer. I've spent too many years seeing them all, the ones who shouldn't even be here, to be expected to just accept them, happy they're around.

I've never been joyful about them, so they have to go.

Once they're all gone, maybe I can find peace.

We'll see.

He goes inside to get changed — he's usually around fifteen minutes in there; I know, I've watched before — so I have a bit of time to think.

* * *

The Past

Alfie stands there with his head hanging low. It's seven o'clock on a Sunday night, and I've had a bellyful of the goings-on lately. Rumours, they spread so quickly, don't they, starting off with a nugget of truth then ending with a load of added extras tacked on, Indian whispers or whatever they're called. That's what I'd thought, anyway, but it seems the extras are the truth after all, going by the state of Alfie.

I'm not sure what to do now I've confronted him. I can't see his expression, what with his face pointing south, so it's difficult to know if I've hit the proverbial nail with my hammering words or whether what I've been told really is a load of old rubbish.

"Look at me," I say. "At least give me that decency."

He raises his head, and it's written all over his face. The rumours, my God, they're true, and he's done something so terrible, so wicked, just because I'm unable to give him what he wants. I wish I could. Wish I could hand him his desire on a gem-encrusted plate, but the universe saw fit to make sure I couldn't, and while he ended up getting what he wanted somewhere else, I'm still left with nothing.

"Please don't tell them I told you," he says. "I promised them I'd keep it quiet."

"Don't tell them? How can I not talk about this with my friends? How can I act as though I know nothing about it, just carrying on our friendship as though I've swallowed a dim-in-the-head pill and I don't believe the rumours? And some friends they turned out to be, carrying on like that behind my back. What I don't understand is why they'd have anything to do with you when you're married to me. Who treats their friend like that? All three of them have broken the trust between us."

"It just happened, love."

"That's what they all say. And don't 'love' me. Maybe you never did. If you loved me, you wouldn't have done it. Wouldn't have behaved in such a shameful manner. Do you even feel guilty?"

"I feel awful."

"Didn't feel awful while you were doing it, though, did you." I fold my arms under my boobs. "You only feel awful because you've been found out. Was it at that party, like people are saying? The one I couldn't go to because I got ill?"

"Yes." His eyes water, his lips wobble.

Good.

"So while I was throwing up all over the place, you were—"

"Honest to God, I'm so sorry."

Oh, you will be. One day you bloody well will be.

"Are they doing anything about it?" I ask.

"No."

My world tilts. I'd have thought they'd have found a solution to their problems, but then again, why should they when they have husbands who'll unknowingly be taking the blame instead?

"Do their old men know about the stories people are telling?" I hope for their sakes they do.

"Not that I'm aware of."

"That's lucky for you then. What if they hear about it, like me?"

"I don't know."

"That's not very helpful, is it. 'I don't know' isn't going to be any good when things start cropping up."

"I can't think that far ahead, love."

"What did I just say about 'love'? Don't you ever call me that again. Don't you ever come near me again like that, *either. We're finished in every way except for living together, presenting some sodding lie to the world that we're a happily married couple. Don't you care what people are saying about me? Whispering in the corner shop? Giggling? I even heard someone say it was* my *fault, that if I was doing it right, you wouldn't have done what you did. Thanks for that."*

"I can't say sorry enough."

"No, you can't. Sorry will never *be enough."*

I walk out then, blinking back tears, my life a wreck because of three things he did that will change everything. Three moments of madness in one night, destroying me for thousands of nights to come.

* * *

He steps out of the changing room in clean grey shorts and a white T-shirt, fancy trainers on, the kind that cost a packet, and jogs towards me, sports bag hanging on his shoulder, just like I knew he would. I step back a bit, hide behind a thick tree trunk, because he'll run past in a minute, taking the trail that leads to the park where I walloped the other fucker. Here he comes, fit as a damn fiddle, unlike the one who came to see me earlier.

He's closer, about two metres in front of me, then he's right here, and I thrust my weapon out, pressing the base of it into the ground. He trips over it, landing flat on his face, saying, "What the . . . ?"

I'll give him what the . . . ?

He rolls onto his back, rubbing his knee. He's caught his shin on a bramble or something. Maybe a sharp stone. Blood dribbles out of a deep gash, meandering down a path between his leg hairs, reaching the top of his white sock within seconds, staining it, creating a semi-colon that's spreading to form the shape of Italy, the toe of the boot long, like clown's shoes. He frowns, possibly thinking he fell over a tree root, and he stares at my weapon, eyes narrowed then going wide.

My angina plays up. Slight twinge to the chest.

He lifts his head, and there I am, right in his line of vision.

"Oh, hello, Auntie!"

Don't you call me that.

"What the hell are you doing out at this time of night, eh? Come to see the match, did you?" He hefts himself up and stands there, concern seeping out of him. "Didn't you hear about Colin? It isn't safe to be out here, and not with your bad leg. This ground isn't exactly even. You can see that because I just fell over."

He points to my weapon. It's similar to an NHS metal crutch, except mine isn't hollow. It's heavy. I filled it with small metal balls. It's good for beating the life out of people.

He gives me a look of such sympathy I want to wipe it off his face. I don't need his sympathy. His very existence has ruined my adult years, and I'm getting on now and want the remaining time I have left to be filled with happiness not bitterness. Smiles not frowns.

"I could say the same to you." I grin, false teeth clacking, damn them. "Didn't *you* hear about Colin?" My nasty glare comes out to play, and I use it to my advantage, creating enough space between us so I can get a good swing of my crutch when the moment is right.

"Yes, I did hear about him, of course I did. I just said something similar to you." He scratches his head as though he's a few jugglers short of a circus.

Probably thinks I'm going senile.

"Then *you* shouldn't be out, should you," I say. The thick bastard doesn't get it, does he.

"Why not?"

"Because you have a connection to Colin."

"Yeah, he's Auntie Beryl's kid. So what?"

"A stronger connection than that."

"Eh?" He makes a face, one that shows he hasn't got a clue what I'm talking about.

I ponder on whether to give him that clue.

No. I don't think so.

Instead, I hit him with my crutch same as I did Colin, chanting in my head with every strike — *I. Fucking. Hate. You. So. Much.* — and he goes down, on his side, the foetal position the final taunt that sends my rage skyrocketing.

Not so fit now, is he.

I lose count of how many times I batter him, but when he doesn't move, when a wheeze then a rattle grates out of his mouth, and his chest fails to rise and fall, my job is done.

Thank the Lord I didn't have to strangle this one.

It takes a long while to walk to the park — I'm spent, physically and emotionally knackered, and my chest hurts, more than a twinge now. Kneeling, glad of a chance to rest, I wash my crutch in the stream, getting the worst of it off in case I bump into anyone; maybe those coppers are still hanging around Starling Road. A few sprays of blood had splattered on me back there, hot and evil on my skin, so I cup my hands in the stream, splashing my face. My coat, that'll be all right. It can be cleaned easily enough. I walk home past where Colin karked it. The only evidence anything was amiss is a strand of police tape fluttering on a bush beside the water. A bit like the Asda tape on those nappies.

I remember then, while crossing the bridge, that the nappies didn't have that tape on the packet when I got them home. I think about whether I touched it, then remember I wore gloves, like I have tonight.

Nothing to worry about then.

CHAPTER FOURTEEN

Tracy stepped inside the station, glad of the warmth compared to outside, tired after a fitful night, her dreams full of Lisa and the hassle she could cause if she didn't sod off out of the picture. Damon had noticed — they lived together now instead of renting two separate places like they had in the city — mentioning she'd kicked out at him a few times. She must have been fighting in her sleep. Probably warding off her father, and John, her old chief, a man who'd shown her 'love' as a child — a love she hadn't wanted.

The only words for it? Sexual abuse, no love about it.

She debated whether to go and visit Vic on the front desk, see if he had any news for her that had come in overnight, left for him to relate to her from the sergeant who manned the desk in the dark hours. She ought to, really, but fancied getting another coffee down her neck before tackling anything. The one she'd had at home hadn't done a thing to perk her up.

A Winter coffee, that would be nice.

She headed up the three flights of stairs after Damon. He went left into the incident room, she went right to Winter's corridor. It was still early, a few minutes until eight when the rest of the team would turn up, so she could afford a natter with the chief. Besides, she wanted Winter to tell her what was going on with Kane, except she'd have to act surprised or nonchalant and make out she hadn't heard any of their conversation.

At his door, she knocked then entered at his call to come in. He stood at the filing cabinet, staring at his coffee maker, the carafe thankfully full, just intermittent drops dripping in from the filter.

"Morning, sir." She smiled as brightly as she could and shifted her focus to the machine.

"I knew I shouldn't have offered you a coffee the first time." He grinned. "Let me give you that link now before you drink my stash dry. I forgot to send it before." He moved to the desk, scribbled on a pad, and ripped the page off. "Here you go."

"Thanks." She folded then slid it into her pocket.

"You want one, I take it?" He raised his eyebrows.

"That's what I'm here for. You can smell it down the corridor." She sat once he'd gestured for her to take a seat, crossing her legs at the ankles and thinking how sad it would be to get on his bad side if he found out about Lisa.

He poured the drinks, and she kept her mouth shut until he'd settled behind his desk. The first sip had her closing her eyes and wishing she was in sunny climes drinking it on a balcony overlooking a beach instead of this cold, austere office in a dreary UK town.

"Do you want to start?" he asked.

"May as well." She took a deep breath. "Kane turned up early evening yesterday. He was on Nada's computer — no one else was around. He closed the browser window, but not before I saw what he was doing. An electoral roll website — one-nine-two dot com. I guessed he was searching for Charlotte Rothers, given the information I received from a team member yesterday — don't think you need to know who that is, do you?"

"No, I don't. Yes, he was looking for Charlotte. He still is. I told him to take a month off. If he steps on any toes belonging to the Cornwall police, that's his problem. I've warned him, but I doubt he'll listen. He wouldn't go into detail, said he couldn't, but he doesn't believe the Pickins/Cobbings' case is over. Okay, it's over in that Pickins is dead and Cobbings is in the nick, but as far as Charlotte goes, he thinks she's up to something. What that is, I have no clue."

Tracy shrugged. "Can't say I'm not happy, because I am. It gets him out of my hair, the team's hair, and he can slay whatever demons he has, and we don't get any repercussions from it. I was concerned about him creating obstacles for us if he stayed on the squad, but with him off in Cornwall, it suits me down to the ground."

"Indeed. Any further forward with the case?" He scratched his earlobe.

"It hasn't thrown up anything of significance so far, no. Well, nothing that points to a suspect anyway. Colin Spinks was a family man who rarely went out other than to work. He spent the evenings and weekends with Natasha Moss, his fiancée, and their daughter." A glimmer of remorse flickered in her chest at the thought of baby Libby growing up without her father. She snuffed it out. "I spoke to two employees at the dry cleaners Spinks runs, and they had nothing to report other than Spinks was liked and wouldn't hurt a fly, that kind of thing." She sipped, loving the taste of the creamer Winter had added, different to the milk from last time. "Where do you buy those little cream tubs from, sir?"

He laughed. "From the same site as the coffee. New, not seen them on there before. Glad I spotted them. So, anything else not coffee related?"

Tracy ran a hand through her hair. "Spinks was on Facebook, but nothing came up from the friends Erica telephoned. They hadn't seen him in years and didn't speak to him much on social media."

"Dead end there then."

"Unfortunately, yes. Nada and Erica were going to see Natasha's father and sister last I spoke to them yesterday, so I'll get an update on that when I meet with the team in a minute. Maybe we'll get leads from those interviews, who knows."

"That would be handy."

"It would. Spinks' mother, Beryl, had a heart attack when we visited her yesterday with the news, so she's in hospital still, as far as I know."

"Good grief. I'll find out how she is, save you doing it. What a shame. The shock, I take it?"

"I'd say so. She thought he'd just taken off for a bit of alone time, even though that was unlike him. She'd gone out into Starling Road to look for him, but no neighbours saw her doing it. There's another old lady who lives next door to Beryl, a Hilda Jones, who is an absolute bear of a woman who I don't want to have to speak to again if I can help it. Bit of a boorish type, if you know what I mean. That's about it, really. Oh, and I need to see what Nada came up with after visiting Asda, where Spinks went to buy nappies before his death. Tim ran the house-to-house in Starling Road where Spinks and Moss live. Ah, yes, and the only thing that came up was someone seeing Hilda Jones walking down the street around the time of the murder, and she told me she wasn't even there, she was at home watching her soaps. I'm thinking the neighbour mistook her for Beryl Spinks."

"So a lot of things going on but they seem to lead nowhere."

"Correct." She took a few swallows of coffee then rose, placing her cup on the filing cabinet. "I suppose I'd better get to it, then. Thanks for the drink."

"You're welcome. Don't make it a habit." He smiled wide.

"Speak to you soon, sir."

She left, buzzing from the caffeine, and pushed open the incident room door. All the team were at their desks, their chairs facing the centre, everyone having a chinwag over vending machine coffee that did nothing to wake you up of a morning or keep you ploughing through the day. Well, it hadn't done anything for Tracy yesterday.

"Morning," she said.

A smattering of greetings ending in 'boss' followed, and she stood in front of the whiteboards to address them. "Sorry to interrupt your conversation, but we need to get updated so we're all on the same page." She repeated what she'd told Winter, plus the fact that Louise Vale, Hilda Jones, and Beryl Spinks all worked at the dry cleaners. Then she asked, "So, Nada, what were the amount of fingerprints estimated for the receipt and the Asda tape?"

"As you can imagine, boss, quite a few. We'll be lucky if we get minimal prints, which, in an ideal world, would enable us to narrow it right down. The manager said several people could have touched the tape. Staff, even cleaners when they go behind the till and dust the shelves. Could have lifted the tape roll to wipe underneath it." Nada sighed.

"What about Moss' father and sister — how did that go?"

"The father wasn't in, so I rang him. He was round at Natasha's with the mother, so we went there. Mr and Mrs Moss are no longer married, but they get on well enough from what I could gather. Seems it was an amicable split. They both just want to be there for Natasha, that much was clear. The father got on well with Colin, didn't have a bad word to say about him."

"Hmm." Tracy rubbed her chin. "Seems everyone liked him. The sister?"

"She was a nice woman. Lives three doors away from Natasha as it happens. She saw Colin walk past on his way to Asda — she was closing her living room curtains, and he waved at her, smiled. The time matches what Natasha told us. The sister liked him, too, was pleased Natasha had found someone decent."

"Damon had the idea this was just random," Tracy said. "What are your thoughts on this, team?"

Shrugs. Mumbles.

"Okay . . . Tim, did you get anything more from the evening stint on house-to-house?"

"Nothing except what Nada just said about Natasha's sister." He kind of winced. "Apologies."

"No worries — and sorry I missed your call, by the way, Tim. Right, with Beryl Spinks in hospital, no leads from Facebook, nothing from Spinks' employees or Natasha's family, ages to wait for the prints to come back, Colin's phone being analysed, his laptop . . ." Tracy raised her hands then dropped them to her sides. "What the hell? I'm still waiting on Gilbert's postmortem findings, but we already know Spinks was battered and strangled. We have nothing." She ground her teeth in frustration. It hurt. "Okay. Keep digging. There's got to be something. I'm going to visit Natasha Moss and her mother again with Damon, see if Natasha is in a better frame of mind to tell us things. I'll be in my office attending to any mail first. Damon, help Tim out with putting together all the Starling Road information for a bit. Thanks, everyone." She paused. "Lara, can you join me in my office for a moment, please." She left, striding down the corridor and into her room.

At her desk, she sorted through envelopes while waiting. Lara came in, her expression showing confusion and a bit of trepidation.

Tracy waved her to the spare seat. "Nothing to worry about, Lara. Park your arse."

Lara sat, hands in her lap, fingers knitted. "Have I done something wrong, boss?"

"God, no. Like I said, nothing to worry about. I want to know how you are, that's all, after our conversation yesterday."

"Oh. Um . . . I'm err . . ."

"Not doing too well?"

"To be honest, I nearly didn't come in today."

Tracy had an idea why, but she asked anyway. "Why's that?"

"He . . . Kane came round last night. Finished it once and for all. I'd been expecting it, but . . ."

"I can imagine. Want to talk about it?"

"I'm okay . . . ish. Wasn't a shock, not really. But he apologised, admitted he'd used me on the rebound, so that's something. He doesn't want us to fall out, and I agreed to meet up with him as friends in the Orange Pebble and be fine with him at work — if he ever comes back."

"The Orange Pebble a pub, is it?"

"Yes. It's on the same estate as Starling Road and the like, out of the way of the station, so no one from work would have seen us together. I should have realised from us always meeting there he'd never want our relationship out in the open. Not that a shag every now and then is a relationship."

"True. What did you mean, 'if he ever comes back'?"

"He's putting in for a transfer."

"To Cornwall."

"How did you know?"

"It was obvious. I saw him before you did yesterday. Told him a couple of home truths. He'd never have settled working with me as his superior. Shame, because we could do with him on the team, couldn't we? But I'd rather not have him if he was going to be half-arsed about everything or going gung-ho every five minutes. No, we have a great team here now, and I was thinking . . . Alastair didn't make it onto this squad, but what do you think of him? Good, is he?"

"Very good. He finds leads where it seems there aren't any."

"Like we're dealing with now." Tracy nodded. "I'm going to give him a trial run on this case. Makes sense that you all remain as one team. Erica's taken Kane's place, and that's all the spots filled, but I'm going to clear it with Winter and get Alastair back for a while, see how it goes. He can go over everything we've gleaned so far. Who knows, he might come up with something. Anyway . . ." She paused. Smiled. "We got off track. Do you need to go home? Take a couple of days? It's not ideal — I'd prefer you to get stuck in and help us out so we can all bond as a team — but if you're really not in the right headspace . . ."

"No, no, I'll stay. I'm half over Kane anyway after that notebook business. I'll take a man break like you suggested then dive back in, see what fish my hook pulls up."

“Good for you. Right, if you want to go back over that CCTV with one of the others, that would be great. I don’t think you’re going to find anything, though, because I reckon the person waited for him at the park, away from any cameras, but we need to double-check just the same so we can put that area properly to bed.”

“All right, boss. And thanks. For . . . you know. Being all right and not the bitch you make out.”

Tracy laughed and threw an eraser at her as Lara left the room, pleased the woman had come down off her high horse and wanted to be a team player instead of Kane’s lapdog.

Maybe this squad would settle down quicker than she’d thought after all.

CHAPTER FIFTEEN

Tracy had her request granted, and Alastair was on loan to the squad for a week to see if he could help find a breakthrough. She'd given him a brief overview of everything and, of course, he had the whiteboard and the other team members to go to should he need anything clarified.

Everyone else got along with sifting through the limited information again in the hope something would stand out as a potential lead, however small.

In her office to once again tackle the mail, Tracy cursed at the interruption of the phone ringing. She snatched it up and almost barked "What?" but thought better of it and gave a polite "Hello?" instead.

"Vic, boss."

"Brilliant. Got something for me, have you?"

"Erm, yes, but not to do with the Spinks case."

Bugger it.

"Okay, what do you have?"

"You're not going to like it, and now I come to think of it, it *might* have something to do with the Spinks case. I'm browsing the info again, and it seems—"

"Do you *like* making people wait, Atkins?"

"Um, sorry, boss. Another murder. Same sort of thing. Head bashed in."

"What?" Tracy's mind spun in a direction she didn't want it to go. Lisa was back on the scene, and suddenly two people had been killed. All right, Lisa's MO had been stabbing before, gutting her victims, but she might have changed her tactics so it didn't raise any red flags. But a bright crimson pennant flapped away in Tracy's head, and she had to suck in a deep breath to combat the sweep of nausea floating around in the back of her throat.

"Boss?"

"Sorry. Um, okay. Where is the victim?"

"Just inside the woods bordering the recreation grounds," he said. "It links to the park where Mr Spinks was found."

Jesus Christ . . .

"Right. Closest road to it, please," she said. "I'll stick the address in the satnav, save you trying to explain where it is." She'd get to know these streets eventually, this town, but at the moment it was like running through a maze, blind as to which direction to take.

Vic gave the details.

"Gilbert been informed?" she asked.

"Just about to do that now, boss."

"Fine. Thank you. I'm on my way." She had a thought. "Oh, before you go — who called it in?"

"Dog walker again."

"Great! Just what we need." Word was going to get out, and a load of mutts were going to be going without walks at this rate, plaiting their damn legs because people would be too afraid to go out. She closed her eyes briefly. "Uniforms there already?"

"Yes, boss."

"Good. Thanks. Talk soon."

She put the phone down and rushed out of her office and into the incident room. "Damon, you're with me."

The team all turned to look at her, some frowning, others with eyebrows raised.

"We've got another fresh one," Tracy said.

Nada winced. "Blimey, boss, that's a bit harsh."

"Sorry. I say it how it is. Get used to it." She clapped once to put an end to more chatter from anyone else who had the idea of butting in. "Same MO. I really didn't want a serial to deal with, but it's looking like that's what's on our plate. We eat what we're served, so to speak, whether we like the fare or not. It happened at the recreation grounds, in the woods, so can you sort it amongst yourselves who's going to switch from what you're doing and get the CCTV footage for that area sent to us. I don't care who does it, just get it done. I'll let you know the victim's name if I can when I'm there so you can get things started with regards to looking into their background. Right, I'm off. Catch you later."

She left, Damon tagging behind, and they made it to the recreation grounds within five minutes, Tracy thanking every deity out there that the roads were relatively free of traffic.

In the car park, they suited up in the white gear and gloves then headed over to Newson, who stood in front of police tape tied around two tree trunks a few metres apart. She nodded at him then signed the crime scene log. While Damon did the same, she scanned the area to get her bearings from the tree line. On the other side of a grass football pitch were Astro Turf pitches or tennis courts, she couldn't tell from so far away and hadn't taken any notice when they'd walked past them just now. Beside those stood two buildings, one white, one brick.

"What are those for?" she asked Newson, pointing.

"Club house and changing rooms," he said. "There was a charity match here last night — five-a-side football — but not many turned up to watch, according to the bloke who runs the bar. Probably because it's cold out."

"Okay. Did you get a list of people who played in the match from the barman?"

"Some. He didn't know all of them. He also mentioned a few of the other customers he knows by name. Others he just knows by sight."

"Brilliant. Give them to DS Hanks here, will you. And where's the dog walker?"

"In the club house," Newson said.

"Okay. Have you questioned them?"

"Yes. He said much the same as the woman who found Mr Spinks."

"Okay, thanks. Assuming you got his name and address, let him know he can go home. I'll contact him later."

A car drew up beside the Astro area, and Tracy squinted, hoping it wasn't the press or some random nosy parker. She recognised the top of the man's head as he got out of the driver's side. Gilbert was here. Good.

He ambled across the grass pitch, and she walked to meet him in the middle.

"Good morning," he said. "But not so good for the victim." He winked.

"Good morning to you, too, and no, not so good. I haven't gone into the woods to see yet, so we'll go in together, shall we?"

Gilbert nodded. "SOCO aren't that far behind me, so let's get a butcher's before everyone else pokes their hooters in."

They strode towards Newson and Damon.

"You're fast becoming one of my favourite people, you know," she said to Gilbert.

"Why's that? It's my jokes, isn't it. Please tell me it's the jokes."

"Yes, it's the jokes, as gross as they are. You remind me of Kathy, another medical examiner I worked with. I didn't think I'd miss her, but you *make* me miss her."

"I'm possibly a poor substitute, but I'll do my best to keep you smiling."

Gilbert signed the log, put his whites on, then they walked past a tree where no tape was attached, Damon following. A WPC Tracy hadn't met yet stood a few yards away from the body, her face hidden in shadows, the meagre sunlight not making it through the thick leaf coverage overhead.

"Hi," Tracy said. "DI Collier" — she pointed her thumb at herself — "DS Hanks." She gestured to Damon. "You are?"

"Constable Simone York, ma'am."

"Boss will do. You can go and stand with Newson now, if you like. Thank you."

Simone appeared glad to be going and shot off, her shoes scuffing fallen leaves and mulch. Tracy cringed at the lack of care at a scene. She'd have a word with Simone's sergeant and ask him to make a point of hammering home how careful PCs needed to be in such circumstances.

"Well, bugger me," Gilbert said, diverting her attention to him. "What a lack of light. I'll have to wait for SOCO to arrive with the big torches to do a proper body check. I've only got a small flash in my bag, but I think it'll do for now."

"We've got one each on our belts," Tracy said and turned to Damon to indicate he should access his. She unhooked hers then switched it on.

The three of them concentrated their beams on the mound of the body ahead.

"Oh dear," Gilbert said. "Someone would have had an almighty headache before he popped his clogs."

Damon turned away, hand over his mouth.

"Go over there for a bit, get those names of the football players and drinkers after the game to Nada," she told him, concerned for him but at the same time trying not to laugh at Gilbert. Was it the severity of the situation that did this? Had her wanting to crack up until her ribs hurt? "We shouldn't joke, really, Gilbert."

He offered her a wan smile. "No, but I can't get through this sort of thing without dropping a funny or two. I do care, you know, more than it seems. This sort of thing" — he held his hand palm up, gesturing at the victim — "has the ability to break you. I don't want to break, I want to find out how they came to be here, so the families get some answers and can begin to move on."

"I understand. I do." She patted his arm. "So, come on, let's get some sort of idea of what happened."

Tracy took in the body. Male, going by the hairy lower legs, revealed as the deceased had shorts on. White socks, some blood on one, a gash on his shin. Trainers that cost a bob or two if the brand was anything to go by, and a white T-shirt, burgundy-spattered, the pattern resembling tie-dye. A bag rested beside him, black sports holdall, the zip done up, blood on the white tick on the side.

Gilbert shone his torch around the victim. "Can't see any obvious evidence, but I'll put a plastic sheet down just in case."

He took one out of his bag, placed it beside the body, then knelt. He stood his torch on the sheet, the beam like a headlamp, the slice of illumination showcasing a face covered in blood and a head that appeared much the same as Spinks' had. To Tracy's eye, it was the same killer, but she wouldn't count her chickens just yet. In the past, one of the little fuckers had run away, and she'd been left waiting for her to reappear ever since.

And now she has.

"Dear God," Gilbert said. "The pain he must have . . ."

"I was just thinking the same. Would it have been quick, the death?"

"Quick enough, but the agony endured beforehand doesn't bear thinking about. This is one set of wounds stitches and paracetamol wouldn't cure had he lived. Brain damage is a given. He wouldn't have had a good quality of life."

Tracy swallowed. "So, two male victims."

"Look in his bag for ID. I'll check his shorts pockets."

Tracy crouched and unzipped the bag, her glove catching on one of the silver teeth. She directed her torch inside. Football boots, the kind without big studs, pink, three black stripes on the side and PREDATOR stamped in gold. Another pair of shorts, black, polyester. Football socks, white, and a sports top, black, white stripes on the arms, the white brand logo a three-piece mountain on the left side of the chest. A shower gel and shampoo combo bottle rested on its side. She dug beneath the clothing, shoved the boots aside, to find a towel, damp and scrunched up where he must have had a shower prior to heading home.

Only he hadn't got there.

Shit.

"Nothing here," she said.

"I've got a wallet and a phone — Sony, android. Let's see now." Gilbert opened the wallet and inspected the contents. "Three credit cards, a debit, National Insurance, driver's license, a fiver in cash, all belonging to a male, forty-one — actually born a week after Spinks if memory serves."

"That's weird," Tracy said. "Name?"

"Francis Vale."

"*What*?" Tracy's heart skipped several beats, and she almost lost the battle in remaining upright. "Say that again?"

"Francis Vale."

She stared at the body, clutching her torch so tight her fingers hurt. "Fuck me sideways."

"I would," Gilbert said, "but you're with Damon."

She couldn't laugh if she tried. "I know that name. There's a woman connected to Spinks, a Louise Vale. She works in his shop once a week. Older lady. I spoke to her on the phone yesterday. Abrupt." Gilbert didn't need this information, but Tracy couldn't stop it tumbling out. "I've got a damn lead at last." She shook her head to chase away the fogginess that had descended, threatening to shut off her ability to think, but the thought crowded into her mind that this couldn't be Lisa — Lisa had chosen random people, no connection whatsoever. *Unless she's upped her game.* Tracy pushed to her feet. "I'll . . . I'll need to take that phone and wallet."

Gilbert stood and grasped her elbow. "Are you all right?"

"Yes, yes, I will be in a minute." Was it relief that it might not be Lisa who had done this creating the light-headedness? Or the fact she'd forgotten to eat breakfast? "It's just a bit of a shock, realising so soon that the deaths are related. That doesn't usually come to light until we've been rooting around for information for a while."

"Well, you've bypassed several steps then, and that can only be good. You'll catch whoever did this quicker." Gilbert took two small plastic bags out of his medical case and popped the wallet and phone into them. "Here. Go and catch a killer."

"Here's hoping we do." She wiped her sweaty brow with her sleeve. "I'll leave you to it." She glanced out to where Damon stood with Newson, past them to the car park. "SOCOs are here."

"Then Francis is in good hands. Off you go now." Gilbert patted her shoulder. "This must be the first time I don't feel like sending someone away with a joke ringing in their ears." He frowned. "I have a feeling there's more to come."

"You and me both, and that feeling's making me want to puke." She smiled and left him there, walking out onto the grass, squinting from the sun that had suddenly decided to make an appearance between patches of thick cloud puffs. Relieved to be away from that poor man whose life had been cut off halfway through the journey to old age, she told herself she had to do what Gilbert had said. Go and catch a killer.

Before they strike again.

CHAPTER SIXTEEN

Out on the grass pitch, Tracy pulled her phone out of her pocket and dialled the incident room, informing Nada of the second victim's name and his connection to Colin Spinks. She shivered from the chill of the eerie sensation that this case wasn't going to be cut and dried. With Gilbert thinking the same thing, it just intensified her suspicions.

"So there you have it," she said. "I can't wrap my head around it at the moment."

"Bloody hell, boss," Nada said. "This is getting nasty."

"It is. Someone's got a serious beef, so we need to find out who the hell they are before they do someone else in. Oh, and Vale and Spinks are the same age, born a week apart. Look into that yourself, will you? Ask the rest of the team to poke into Vale's background. Leave Alastair to get on with what he's already doing, though, all right?"

"Yes, boss."

"We're going to see Louise Vale now." Tracy slapped her forehead. "Piss. I left her address on a pad on my desk. Can you nip in there and read it out to me?"

"Yep. Won't be a minute."

A clonk sounded, Nada putting the phone on the desk most probably, and Tracy tapped her foot, impatience souring her blood, turning it hot, chasing that eerie chill away, her cheeks heating. Why hadn't Nada taken the handset with her to save time, for God's sake?

Tracy turned to catch Damon's attention, waving him over, and he nodded to Newson then joined her.

"You okay?" she asked, concerned he still suffered when viewing dead bodies. After the case involving Lisa, she thought he'd be over that particular phobia by now.

"Yeah. It's worse than before. You know, seeing them. I can stop myself puking, but the fear, knowing that could have been me being laughed at by the likes of Gilbert and Kathy. Since that woman stabbed me . . ."

"I know. Don't go there." *Please don't keep reminding me of what Lisa did.* "And Kathy and Gilbert *have* to laugh to get through it. Can you imagine how many postmortems they do in a week? It's got to mess with your head — and your heart. Actually, I know it does. The pair of them have admitted as much to me. So let them deal with it the way they have to, even if you don't agree with it or understand it. We all have to cope the best way we know how. Take me and my life. See what I mean?"

He nodded.

"Oh, hold on." She held her hand up.

"There wasn't an address, boss," Nada said, panting from where she must have been darting about, "just a phone number, so I looked her up. This case is just getting weirder than a three-pound coin."

"What do you mean?" Tracy held her breath.

"She lives in Robin's Way."

"You're joking." What the fuck was going *on* here?

"Err, no, boss. Wish I was."

"What number?"

"The other side of Beryl Spinks. Number nineteen."

"What? So we have Louise Vale, nineteen, Beryl Spinks, twenty, and that wretched Hilda Jones, twenty-one, all in a row?"

"There's got to be something in that, boss."

"Too right there has. Get on it, Nada, right away. But before you go, check whether Francis Vale has a next of kin that isn't his mother. Quick as you can." That clonk of the phone came once more, and Tracy congratulated herself on not fucking up again and visiting Louise Vale without checking for a wife first.

It seemed ages until Nada got back on the line. "Yes, a wife, Olivia, and stranger still, she lives in Starling Road, number eleven, next door to Alison Imers, the woman who said she saw Hilda Jones in the street the night Colin Spinks was killed."

"Oh, seriously, this is all just creepy bollocks." Tracy rubbed her forehead, trying to recall if Olivia Vale had given any pertinent information during the house-to-house. "Check if she said anything to Tim or the PCs when they questioned everyone in Starling Road, will you? I'll wait."

"Two secs."

More than two secs went by, and Tracy's impatience climbed the ladder from the fourth rung to the top. "Come on, come on."

"Boss?"

"I'm here."

"Olivia saw nothing. She was getting her two sons to bed around eight o'clock. Told them a story until half past, then had a bath. Francis was also questioned — God, isn't that just awful; he didn't have a clue he would be next."

"Just shows how life is so unpredictable, doesn't it?"

"It does."

"Carry on; what did Francis say he was doing?"

"Watching a film. Oh God. This is so poignant, boss. *Die Hard*."

"Oh, fuck me."

"I know . . . I also checked whether Mr Vale was reported as missing — I assume his murder happened last night?"

"Ugh, I didn't even ask Gilbert. I got . . . side-tracked."

"Well, no one called it in, so maybe he stays out overnight often and his wife didn't think anything of it."

"Okay, thanks. We'll be back as soon as we can."

Tracy cut the call and hurried back into the woods. She tapped a busy Gilbert on the shoulder. "Sorry to bother you. Got a time of death estimate for me?"

"About eight. Last night, I'd say. Rigor has come and gone — it wasn't as cold as when Colin was killed. I say come and gone; his torso is still a little rigid, but the rest of him is floppy."

"Cheers."

She rushed out onto the grass, moving towards the car park.

Damon jogged beside her. "Did I hear what I think I just heard? Louise Vale . . . ?"

"Is the mother of the victim back there, Francis Vale."

"Christ. *And* all the old women know each other outside of living in the same street."

"They all work at Spinks' shop one day a week, yes." At the car, Tracy unlocked it and got inside, adrenaline forging an intense path through her veins.

Damon folded himself into the passenger seat and sorted his safety belt. "Do we know if Hilda Jones has a son or daughter?"

"No. But if she does . . ." Tracy guided the car through the entrance between two high hedges then pulled out onto the road, heading for Starling.

"I don't even want to think about the connotations of that," Damon said.

"Well, I'm afraid we've got no choice *but* to think about it. If she *does* have a child, at least we can warn her — and the son or daughter, more if she's had a few kids. First, though, we need to visit Olivia Vale, Francis' wife." She filled him in on what Nada had said about the Vale couple and what they'd done that night.

"That film title, though," he said.

"Indeed. Once we've been to see Olivia, we'll nip to Louise Vale's and give her the news. Here's hoping she doesn't have a heart attack and all."

Let's see if she's more sympathetic about her own son dying than she was about Beryl's. I wonder if Louise will be so keen to get her dinner on tonight after she hears what we've got to say.

"Damn, I'm a bitch," she said, sighing, annoyed with herself for being cruel when she was supposed to be concentrating on being a better person. Maybe she couldn't. Maybe she had to accept herself as she was, flaws and all, wear her Princess Judgmental crown and make the best of it. She turned briefly to look at Damon.

"At times, yes, but it's who you are. I've told you before, I love all the Tracys you've been since I first met you. What's bothering you?"

She told him what had sauntered into her head.

"Ouch. Yeah, that was bitchy." He tapped his fingertips on the door.

"But human, yes? We all think things like that, don't we?"

He shook his head. "I don't."

"Maybe it's only me then, and you're the exception?" But she knew it wasn't just her. "Kathy's a bitch, too, so I'm not alone."

"Perhaps just keep those kinds of thoughts inside," he suggested. "You know, don't let them come floating out of your mouth like you sometimes do."

She could do that — if she tried hard enough. The problem was, the images in her head transferred to words faster than she could catch on to the process, and by then it was too late.

"I'll give it a go," she said, "but you know I'll fail."

"But if you're trying to curb it, that counts for something."

Her chest hurt with how much she loved him. "You're an exceptional man, mister."

"I give it a good go and hope for the best. You do the same. You're much better than you were this time last year, so you've consciously made the effort to do better."

She agreed; she wasn't as acrimonious as she used to be, although at times that could be debated. Maybe the day would come when she thought before she spoke all the time instead of every so often.

"Shit, we're here." She parked in front of number eleven, a three-bed by the look of it, double-glazed windows, white frames, mahogany front door with an arch of stained glass in the top, leaves and butterflies in purple, green, and red.

No accounting for taste.

There she went, doing it again . . .

Dear God, there's a fucking gnome on the doorstep.

Maybe the kids chose it.

A twinge of guilt twisted her stomach, and so she didn't delve into why she felt it, she got out of the car and waited for Damon on the pavement. They walked up the garden path side by side, Tracy's guts churning. Damon grabbed her hand and squeezed it, then let it go. He nodded, and she hoped she could do as he'd suggested while delivering this news and be sympathetic instead of frank.

"Here goes." She pressed the bell button.

A woman answered, auburn hair in a ponytail, a yellow polishing cloth in one hand. "Yes? Can I help you?"

"Hi. Olivia Vale?" Tracy pulled her ID out.

Damon did likewise.

Olivia smiled. "Yes. Is this about Colin? Only, I told that other detective, Tim someone, what we were doing that night."

"It's partly to do with Colin, yes. May we come in?" Tracy smiled, tight-lipped.

"Of course." Olivia stepped back into a slender, beige-carpeted hallway, one hand on the door, the other by her side, the cloth flapping in the breeze that had decided to make itself at home inside. She shivered. "Wow, that's an ill wind."

It is indeed, and we're going to gust right in and blow your happiness away.

Tracy and Damon entered, waiting by the stairs on the right while Olivia shut the door. She led them through to a kitchen on the left, pretty spacious, lemon-coloured walls, beechwood cabinets, silver knobs, a beechwood table and chair set in the dining area.

"Want some tea?" Olivia asked.

"No, thank you," Tracy said, "although feel free to make one for yourself."

You might need it.

"Oh, no, that's fine. I try not to drink too much of it. It's the caffeine. Francis — that's my husband — is a health freak, and he's sold the benefits of water to me. Actually, he should be home in a minute. Shall we wait so you can question us together?"

"Please sit down, Mrs Vale." Tracy willed her speeding heartbeat to slow.

"Oh. Okay . . ." Olivia perched on the edge of a chair and rested her hands on the table, knuckles almost brushing a cut-glass fruit bowl in the centre full of grapes, apples, and a peach or two, a bruise on one of them. Bananas hung from one of those fancy metal stands.

"Where was Francis last night?" Tracy asked.

"He went to a footy match for a charity — he was one of the players — then he was meeting up with a friend who wasn't involved in the match to have a drink in memory of Colin. Francis stayed over at Jim's. Why?"

"Jim who?"

Damon took his notebook out.

"Jim Collins. Look, what's going on?" She frowned and wrung her hands, jolting the table.

The bananas swung.

"Where does Jim live?" Tracy hated doing this just before delivering the News, but if she did it after, she wouldn't get any sense out of the woman.

Olivia recited the address, then, "Is something wrong?"

"Damon, can you pop next door to see if Alison Imers is in?" Tracy waited until he'd gone. "Alison is a friend, yes?"

"Yes, sort of. She's known Francis longer than me. They went to school together. We help each other out with milk and whatever sometimes, small things like that. Our kids go to the same school, they're in the same class, so they play together in either of our back gardens. But we're not as close as that might make you think." She bit her bottom lip. "I'm feeling uncomfortable. Something's happened, hasn't it."

Damon appeared in the kitchen doorway, a woman beside him — blonde, the gym bunny sort, her leggings tighter than the skin of a facelift recipient.

"Um, just give us a moment, will you?" Tracy said to him.

Damon got the message and ushered Alison out, closing the door behind him. He'd bring her back when Olivia screamed the house down, and Alison would be left with the task of mopping up tears and consoling someone it seemed she wasn't exactly best buddies with.

Such is life.

Tracy sat opposite Olivia and took one of her hands in hers. That gesture was a step in the right direction, wasn't it? "I'm so very sorry, but I have to inform you that Francis was killed last night."

She waited for the shock to hit, for the shrieking to start, but it never came. Instead, Olivia laughed. Too hard, too hysterically.

Fuck.

Tracy waited one beat, two beats, and then the tears and racket came, as did Damon and Alison, and Tracy calculated when it would be appropriate to get the hell out and separate herself from the awful grief swamping Olivia Vale like a man's jumper on a three-year-old kid. A FLO would deal with that.

Olivia flailed, her hands rising, knocking the bananas off their stainless-steel gallows, the fruit thudding much like Tracy imagined Francis had when he'd hit the ground.

Time to go.

CHAPTER SEVENTEEN

In Robin's Way, parked outside Mrs Jones', Tracy pulled in a deep breath to steady her nerves. Who should she visit first? Vale or Jones? By rights, it should be Vale, but she couldn't face another barrage of mourning at this moment.

Decision made, she said, "We'll ask Jones if she has any children first." She shut the engine off.

Damon twisted in his seat and stared at her. "Why? It's protocol to—"

"I *know* what the protocol is, damn it, but think about it for a second. Francis is dead, okay? Nothing can help him now. But if Mrs Jones has kids, we'd be better off warning her first so we can prevent another murder."

"If that's even what's going to happen."

"Should we take the chance it won't?"

"I suppose not."

"No suppose about it. You know it makes sense."

"Yep, whatever you say, boss."

That meant he didn't really agree, him using 'boss' like that while they were alone, but Tracy was too wound up to give a shit whether he was on board or not. She got out of the car, straightened her jacket, smoothed her hair, and steeled herself for another hostile conversation with Jones. Honestly, it seemed the woman lived to make talking as uncomfortable as possible.

Damon walked up the path with Tracy, and she knocked, waiting for a few seconds then repeating the action.

"Give her a chance, love," Damon said. "She might be upstairs or on the loo."

The door opened, and Belligerent Bertha herself filled the doorway, a dark-green scouring pad in one hand, washing-up bubbles sitting like aerated frog spawn on the other. What, was it cleaning day on this estate or something?

"Oh, it's you again, Detective Inspector Tracy Collier," Hilda said, mouth turning down at the corners in a sneer. "Haven't you done enough damage? Beryl's still in hospital, did you know that? Fighting for her life, she is. So I heard anyway."

"I'm sorry she took the news so badly. However, her reaction to it isn't my fault." *That's right, I'm not taking the blame for anything I don't have to these days. The Past taught me that.* "I need to ask you a question."

"So long as it isn't going to send me to my grave, fire away."

Sarcastic cow.

Bit like peas in a pod, you two.

Get lost.

"Do you have any children, Mrs Jones?" Tracy smiled, hoping it would soften Hilda a bit.

The woman winced, face screwing up as though she'd eaten fizzy sherbet, then she composed her features to a bored expression. "No."

"Thank f—goodness," Tracy said.

"What do you want to know that for?" Hilda asked, the frog spawn sliding off her hand to plop onto her pink fluffy slipper.

"I'll tell you after I've visited Mrs Vale."

"What do you need to see her for?" She frowned.

"You'll find out shortly."

Tracy turned and left the garden, walking two houses down to number nineteen, coaching herself to get the hell inside, give the news, then leave Jones to deal with the aftermath.

"Same as before, all right?" she said to Damon as they approached Vale's front door. "Actually, I want to get this over and done with as quickly as possible. Go and stand with Jones — she's still on her step, the nosy bugger — and I'll go in here and leave the door on the latch. Give me a minute or two, okay?"

"Righty oh."

Tracy rang the bell, and whom she presumed was Louise Vale opened the door, the fronts of her brown cable-knit cardigan held in place with one arm across her middle. She smiled tentatively, her going-white eyebrows the same colour as her Vera Lynn hair, so many wrinkles on her face it would take all day and then some to count them all. Tracy reminded herself of how rude this woman had been on the phone and hardened her heart a little more than it was already.

"Mrs Vale?"

The old dear nodded, her green eyes turning hazel — with suspicion? "Yes. I'm not buying anything, and I don't want my windows washed. I do them myself with newspaper and vinegar, and my son does the top ones. I don't give to charity because that begins at home, and I'm not into no god or whatever, so if you're collecting for a church, you can sling your hook."

Why are these people sent to try me?

Tracy pasted on a fake smile. It didn't sit right, so she adopted her usual resting bitch face. That felt better. "I'm DI Collier, and I need to come in for—"

Vale's eyes widened. "Ah, so *you're* the one who rang me yesterday and put Beryl in hospital. Proud of yourself, are you, sending a woman halfway to death by telling her about her son dying like that? You ought to be ashamed of yourself."

"I'm afraid it's my job, Mrs Vale." *God grant me the serenity to accept the things I cannot change, courage to change the things I can, and wisdom to know the difference. If you can't manage that, dear Lord, give me permission to slap a granny.* "I don't enjoy it, I assure you."

"You can assure me all you like, but I won't ever believe you."

Tracy sighed. Bristled. Wanted to walk away and leave this job to Nada and Erica. She tried again — one more shot and she was out of there. "I really ought to come in, Mrs Vale. What I have to say shouldn't be done on the doorstep."

"No. I won't let the likes of you in my house. Say what you've got to say out here." She crossed her arms and clasped her elbows, liver spots on the backs of her hands stark on thinning skin. "Then I'll have witnesses, people who can see what's occurring through their windows. I'll tell you something for nothing."

Oh, please do . . .

"Beryl didn't have a dodgy ticker, so for all I know, you did something to her to make her have that heart attack. Can't be too careful around certain folks these days, and you've got unsympathetic scrawled on your forehead in bright colours, so I don't trust you."

Tracy reminded herself that this woman in front of her had some terrible times ahead. Although Vale was acting as if she were sixty or so years younger, a ten-year-old testing the boundaries, it didn't give Tracy an excuse to be rude.

Or maybe it did, but she'd better not.

"I can't do this outside, Mrs Vale." *How am I going to get around this?* "Would you prefer to speak to my colleague instead?"

Vale swivelled her eyes to look over at Damon and Jones. "Oh. I didn't see them there. That him, is it? What's he doing with Hilda?" She scrunched her eyes up as if helping herself to see.

"Yes, that's him. Would you like him to come in?"

She shrugged. Returned her attention to Tracy. Sniffed and pursed her lips for a second. "He'll do. *You* can stay put, though."

"Fair enough."

Tracy called Damon over and met him at the bottom of the garden. She had the urge to bolt, to go home. It didn't really feel like home yet, but it was better than being here. Talk about being thrown in at the deep end so far in this new job. No settling in period, nothing.

"She won't let me in." Tracy canted her head in Vale's direction. "I'm afraid this one's yours." Then she waved at Jones. "I'll send *her* in after you."

"Shit." A muscle twitched in Damon's jaw. He shook his head, seeming as weary as Tracy. "Jones has already been giving me what for. She's unbearable."

"I know, but Vale is more awkward than Jones, and that's saying something." Tracy exited the garden and waited on the pavement.

Damon strode to the front door, said something to Mrs Vale, then went inside with her.

Jones barrelled up, breasts swaying, her tight-bun hairdo obviously dyed now Tracy glimpsed it in natural light. "What do you want, bloody waving at me like that? I've got things to do." She flapped her scouring pad in front of Tracy's face.

"I need you to go inside Mrs Vale's with DS Hanks in a moment," Tracy said.

"All right, but I'm not doing it for you, so don't think you've buttered me up. I'm doing it for him. He's a nice fella. And I'll do it for Lou. She's been a good friend throughout the years."

"How long have you known her and Beryl?" Tracy asked, stalling to give Damon time to break the news.

"More years than I care to count, if you *really* must know." She studied the sky then levelled her gaze on Tracy. "Since before our . . . Before Colin and Francis were born. They arrived in seventy-seven, so . . . hmm, got to be seventy-threeish. Why? What's that got to do with the price of fish?"

"Nothing. Fish doesn't come into the equation, unless you mean the smell of it. You know, something smelling a bit fishy around here."

Jones narrowed her eyes. "What are you insinuating?"

"Not a thing. Where did you all meet?"

"Want to know the ins and outs of everything, you do." Jones sighed. "We worked in a secretarial pool. Been friends ever since."

"What firm was this?" Tracy asked.

"Ace Accountants. It's not around anymore. Used to be down the alley next to Clarks in town. Beside the old warehouses is a small office block. There."

Clarks, the shoe shop, and the warehouses rang a bell. They were from Kane's case.

"I see." Tracy tucked a strand of hair behind her ear. "Why is it no longer around?"

"Owner is dead." Jones swallowed. Seemed as though she didn't want to continue this subject.

Interesting.

"Mrs Jones?" Tracy tapped her foot.

"He . . . he . . . committed suicide." Jones paled.

"In what manner?"

"Threw himself in front of a train."

"Oh dear." *Easy to look that up, then.* "Do you all live so close because you're such good friends?"

Jones blushed — anger? Tracy wasn't sure.

"We live close because we live close, and that's all you need to know. I'll be off with DS Hanks now. I'm telling you, this had better not be a repeat of yesterday, or I'll . . ." She slapped a hand to her chest. "Oh God, it isn't, is it?"

"Thank you for your time, Mrs Jones," Tracy said, then she stalked off to her car, chalking that up as a win in the 'I'm in charge not you' department.

So, the women had known each other a long time, had they, and two of their sons had been killed. Maybe the link wasn't the victims after all, but their mothers. Jones didn't have any children, though, so perhaps the team ought to concentrate on anything going on in the past between Beryl Spinks and Louise Vale. Tracy hadn't expected to be going so far back in time, but she'd do whatever it took to solve this one, her first case in her new role. It needed to be the benchmark for all those that followed.

She couldn't balls this up.

Opening the car door, she flung herself inside and let the latest information sink in, head back, eyes closed, a headache forming. A long friendship like the one these women shared had to have seen some major ups and downs over time. Skeletons in closets had a habit of tumbling out when you least expected it, and whatever had been hidden was well and truly showing itself now. The question was, what the fuck had happened to result in two forty-one-year-old men being killed one night after the other?

She rang Nada and passed on the info, giving her the task of poking into the past to see whether any bones of deception could be uncovered. The stapes would do, the smallest in the human body — after all, once you got hold of even the tiniest piece of evidence, it could blow everything wide open.

Like Mrs Vale's door, which was flung in an arc and crashed into the hallway wall, Jones hefting herself over the threshold to stomp down the garden path, face like a bulldog chewing a wasp.

"Bloody hell . . ." Tracy started the engine so she could lower the driver's-side window.

Jones' face and shoulders filled the frame. "You could have warned me."

Could I now . . . "It wasn't for me to tell you before Mrs Vale had been informed."

"I went in there, and she was crying all over the bleedin' place. What the devil is going on?" Jones thumped the door.

"I'd appreciate it if you didn't do that again, Mrs Jones. Criminal damage and all that. And as for what's going on, that's what we're trying to find out." Tracy glanced at Vale's house. Relieved Damon was coming out, she said, "If you're such good friends, you'll be wanting to go in there to comfort Mrs Vale, won't you."

Damon got in beside Tracy.

"Do you think this has something to do with . . ." Jones glanced up and down the street. "Doesn't matter. I hope to never have to see you again."

Tracy raised the window, and once it closed, said, "Works both ways, you old . . . you infuriating woman."

"Isn't she just," Damon said.

"How did Vale take it?"

"She's distraught, as you can imagine. I've given the number to call for support if either of them need it — some people refuse having a FLO. Hopefully Mrs Jones won't make things worse. Maybe she'll find her compassionate streak beneath all that bluster."

"Stranger things have happened." Glad to have that job over and done with, she drove out of Starling Road. "Got the address for today's dog walker?"

Damon fished his notebook out of his pocket. "Yep."

"Plug it into the satnav, will you? Ta."

Damon pressed buttons to input the location. "Back the other way. It's one street down from Starling."

"Bugger." She turned around and took it slowly. "I'm tired. Think we should stop off somewhere for a coffee first?"

"Have one at the dog walker's."

"If he offers us anything. Some people don't, do they. It's typical. They ask when we don't want one, and when we're gagging, they don't."

"Quick change of subject. Are you worrying about something?" Damon reached across and buried his hands in the hair at the base of her neck.

There was nothing for it but to lie, much as she hated to. Still, the decisions she'd made meant she'd always have to skirt the truth with him. "Only catching the son of a bitch who did this."

"Nothing else?"

"Nope."

"It's just that you really were unsettled last night. Did you get much sleep?"

"Not really. It's a new house. Takes a while to get used to the creaks and groans, doesn't it. Half the time I heard a rattle and thought someone was breaking in. I'm sure in a week or two I'll be okay." *When I know whether or not my fucking sister is on another killing spree.*

"I hope so. I hate to rub it in, but I've slept better since we moved here."

I did, too, until Lisa turned up. "Good. Okay, looks like this is where we need to be. Let's get in there and get out. *Then* we're going for a coffee, the strongest Costa has to offer."

Then she told him about the women working at Ace Accountants, and they mulled over what that could mean, if anything. Sometimes, the most innocent-sounding piece of information turned out to be the biggest lead.

"I let Nada know, so hopefully they'll dig something up," she said.

"Here's hoping."

CHAPTER EIGHTEEN

The Past

Alfie has something to tell me, so he says, and I'm not sure I want to hear it. After the terrible time I've been through recently, having salt rubbed in my open, gaping wounds, I don't think I can take much more.

"What is it now?" I ask, rubbing a streak of dust from my sweaty forehead, staring into the bathroom mirror and wondering just when I got to look so much older than I am.

It was six months ago the first fine wrinkles appeared, from worry, upset, and the rotten thoughts that seem to continually break into my mind, turning me into someone I never thought I'd be. I'm only thirty and have more signs of aging than I expected, naïvely thinking I wouldn't get any until my forties. Beryl and Hilda have smooth skin, but I suppose they would, being five years younger. But even Louise, thirty-two, doesn't have a ravine in sight.

"Something that needs to be discussed," Alfie says.

"I'm tired. Helping those three out has drained me. Leave me alone."

All weekend we've been going to and fro between Hilda's, Beryl's, and Louise's old houses to their new ones, three homes in a row. They're now living on the newest estate in town, though how they've afforded deposits for their mortgages I'll never know. Their husbands don't have amazing jobs, and us girls earn a pittance at Ace Accountants, Alfie's company. We could afford the deposit, Alfie and I, but I'm okay staying where I am, and besides, living in the same street as them would be torturous. I'm barely able to remain polite with them at work, and I've avoided seeing them outside of it until yesterday when Alfie insisted we should show up and give them a hand.

Mind you, they'll all be leaving work soon, and I'm more than capable of running things by myself. I've told Alfie he doesn't need more than one secretary, especially when he can't keep his hands to himself. He wouldn't dare go against what I've said.

I know things — things he wouldn't want me to tell the girls' husbands.

Alfie leans on the doorjamb, arms crossed, his T-shirt smeared with dirt from where he'd carried our gifts into their pristine, posh-as-the-queen houses — indoor plants, something to place on a windowsill or the centre of a table on top of a doily. The girls had gushed as though aspidistra was the best thing they'd ever seen, and I'd just wanted to smack them over their heads with the pots to wipe the false smiles off their pretty little faces.

"Just tell me, get it over with. I need to have a bath and go to bed." I brush my hair, straggly from sweat. I must have lugged over fifty boxes the last two days.

Hilda's husband, William, had said I looked good even in my old clothes, that my slim figure was a sight for sore eyes, and I'd wondered whether every man ogled other people's wives as though they could talk to them any way they pleased.

Do things they shouldn't.

"Next weekend," Alfie says, "We're doing this all over again."

I try to stop the retort coming out, but it's too late. It's on my tongue already. "Helping to move another of your floozies, are we?"

"Pack it in," he says. "That's enough now."

"Enough? Oh, so you just want to forget it all, do you? Expect me to forget it, too? Never. I'll never forget what you've done to me and my friends' husbands. This deception is more than anyone should be expected to put up with, but I happen to have taken my vows seriously, and I'll not walk away. Instead, I'm going to make your life just as much hell as you've made mine."

"I could leave you."

"You could, and I could tell people what you've done."

"We're moving to Robin's Way," he announces, bold as you like. "Number twenty-two. I need to be able to see them regularly."

"See them?" I slap the hairbrush down.

"I can't give them up."

"Oh, this has got to be a joke. You're telling me I have to live *beside them and see them every day, too?"*

"If you wouldn't mind."

"Mind? Mind? Oh, of course I don't mind. Every wife would love to live near people who have the ability to send her to the nuthouse."

"Sarcasm doesn't suit you."

"Shame, because it's my new best friend, haven't you noticed?"

"Yes, unfortunately I have."

"Go away, Alfie."

* * *

The next weekend we move into Robin's Way, and for the following months I keep to myself, while Alfie goes round to their houses in the evenings for various parties, dinners, and quiet drinks. He rubs along well with their husbands, and one night, while Alfie is at a get-together for the lot of them at Beryl's, William, Hilda's old man, turns up on my doorstep, wanting to know why I never join them.

I ask him to come inside, leading him to the living room. "Oh, parties aren't my thing. Parties can cause a lot of trouble." I'm feeling him out, seeing what he knows.

"So I heard," William says.

"You did?"

"Yes."

"So why do you let him into your home?"

"He paid all our deposits."

"What?"

Alfie earned a lot of money, but enough to afford four *deposits, theirs and ours? Was he scamming someone he did the accounts for? I'll have to have a look at the various books when I'm next in the office.*

"It was a stipulation of mine," William says.

I blink, shocked that he knows, amazed he's going along with this lie, same as me. "Do the other men know?"

"Not that I'm aware."

"Oh."

"Make me a drink, will you? A stiff one."

I move over to the wooden globe drinks cabinet and pour him a vodka and tonic. When I hand it to him, his fingers brush mine, and I find myself seeing him as if for the first time. He's good-looking, his dark hair long, the opposite to Alfie's short blond style, his fashionable sideburns curly, Alfie clean-shaven.

"Fancy a revenge fuck?" William asks, taking the drink and tossing it down his throat.

I struggle not to stagger backwards. I manage to hold my ground, shaking, anger growing in a slow boil.

"It's not like anyone will know, is it," he says. "You can't get pregnant."

He laughs, too loud and too harsh, and I slap his face.

"Get out, and don't come back here. I'm not like your wife. Not like the other two, either. They're disgusting, and I'm only polite to them because of Alfie."

William slams the glass on the coffee table. Rubs his cheek over the red finger marks I put there. "Why bother? It's not like he's been giving you the same consideration all this time."

I don't know why I'm staying. Maybe it's the stigma of divorce. Maybe it's because I won't find anyone else to take me, a barren woman, unable to provide the family most men want.

"It's none of your business why I bother," I snap. "Please leave now."

He walks to the living room door then stops. "If that kid is born with blond hair, you won't see me for dust."

William leaves, and I stand here, tears burning, thinking of how I'm stuck in this awful situation. The ridiculousness of it all strikes me then, and I laugh like William did, hating the way it sounds but unable to stop the noise coming out of me.

It's the seventies, supposedly a time of free love, smoking weed and letting it all go, but some of us are still stuck in fifties values, and walking out on your husband just isn't done.

No, you just have to grin and bear it.

* * *

The baby came out blond.

The baby came to live with us.

I'm its mother now.

William has left Hilda, has moved to Scotland, and she's told everyone her husband died and she lost the baby. Except it isn't lost, it's here, in my arms, while I sit on our bed trying to shut the little shit up. He represents everything I could never give birth to myself, a symbol of my husband's infidelity, my friends' disloyalty, a taunt, a reminder each and every day that I'm a failure in so many ways.

I hate the baby.

I hate Alfie.

I hate myself.

But I hate my friends more.

* * *

The doorbell rings, and I plonk the boy in his crib then go downstairs to see who wants a piece of me now. I'm tired from the child wailing all night, the stupid thing trying to get milk from a breast that's empty and will never fill to provide nourishment for the likes of him. He hasn't taken to the bottle and spews more out than what goes in.

Alfie is at work, probably hands-on with his new secretary, while I'm stuck at home near the fruits of his sexual labours, resentful, bitter, and wishing I could end it all now, that my plan wasn't so far into the future. I can hardly wait for the years to zip by so I can do what I have to do.

I swing the door open, and there's Beryl and Louise with their blond baby sons — quiet, good baby sons who feed nicely, sleep nicely, and do every-bloody-thing nicely. Beryl and Louise don't look as though they've been dragged through a hedge backwards, whereas I could pass for Yeti's wife.

It's the weekly get-together, and I forgot. I have no clue what day it is most of the time, but it must be Tuesday as they're here.

I let them in and say the baby upstairs is sleeping, although he's probably getting ready to squawk the house down at any moment.

Beryl and Louise bustle about in my kitchen, making the tea and telling me to have a seat and a breather. Then Louise trit-trots out to answer yet another peal of the doorbell. Hilda waddles in, still looking pregnant, and I wish she'd have the guts to take her baby back and stick two fingers up at those who would frown on her being a single mother.

I wish I had the guts, too, to leave Alfie and start again.

But I don't want to now. I want revenge more. I'm going to make each and every day unbearable for him, just as I promised. I'll suffer with that horrible baby in the upstairs crib. Suffer the intolerable tea mornings with these three. I'll lull every single one of them into a false sense of security, then I'll strike and send them all to Hell, the place I live every second, every minute, every hour of every day.

Patience is a virtue.

The child in the bedroom wails, and Hilda rushes up there, as she always does. Tuesdays are the days she can play mother to her child, where everyone here knows the score and won't tell a soul. Where we've pretended we've forgotten the conversation when I confronted them all in the pub and told them I knew what was going on.

I can tell when Hilda has picked him up because he stops crying, whereas if I pick him up, he doesn't.

Bloody little bastard.

Hilda brings him down and lays him on the blanket on the floor beside his brothers. They could be triplets, all born within two weeks of each other, all with the same features. Louise and Beryl still have their husbands, who don't seem to have a clue that some other dog snuck into their yard and fucked their bitches.

I stare at Alfie's sons.

How it is possible to detest innocent beings?

I don't know, but I detest them.

One day, they won't exist, like they should never have existed in the first place.

One day, these three women, these so-called friends of mine, will understand my pain.

And one day, Alfie will reap what he's sown — they all will.

Until then, I'll play make-believe, I'll live the lie, and I'll smile.

Hilda breaks into my musings and tugs me over into the corner. "People have been asking how you had a baby but didn't show." She points to my flat stomach.

"I don't care what they're saying."

"I told them he was mostly in your back. You know, some people carry babies that way, barely a bump."

"I wouldn't know," I say.

"Sorry."

"You should have been sorry a long time ago."

She trudges off to her son, kneeling beside him and stroking his soft cheek. Hilda sings a tune, and the child gurgles, smiles, happy and content.

He'll pay for that.

CHAPTER NINETEEN

Notes:
When their death is likely to bring such pain you can taste it, then you know it was a job well done. That's what I'm hoping for. Pain I can taste.

That policewoman and her brawny sidekick have gone now, so I leave the house to go to Louise's. At last, I can witness the results of my hard work, of all those years living in pain, tortured by events out of my control. But Beryl having that heart attack wasn't something I'd imagined happening, I can tell you. I've been short-changed.

Story of my life.

I move along the street, tapping my weapon on the very pavement Colin and Francis have walked on, and feel nothing but relief that I won't have to see them walking on it ever again. No more smiles to witness, those boys striding up the paths of their childhood homes to greet their mothers with hugs and flowers, chocolates sometimes, too. No more seeing Alfie's grandbrats gallivanting in the front gardens, playing ball and kicking it into the street, likely to cause an accident. I can't see Francis' wife popping round for a cuppa with Louise. Last I heard, she couldn't stand her mother-in-law.

And just think, no more seeing Colin's dribbly shit of a daughter, either, unless that Moss girl brings her round.

No more of anything once that other little bastard has been taken care of.

That'll be done tonight.

I'm at Louise's door, and I suppose she might think it's odd me coming here, seeing as I stopped talking to her and Hilda after Alfie's fortunate date with that train. For some reason I've remained in contact with Beryl. Something tells me she wasn't . . . complicit in what happened back then, though I can't put my finger on why. Still, I'll make out I'm giving support for old time's sake.

Hilda answers, and her face is a picture, full of shock and worry.

Worry you might, woman, because you're thinking about what could be coming next, aren't you.

I offer the expected sad expression, which is difficult considering I want to laugh until my sides split. I long to rub it in, say to them: *Payback is a bitch, isn't it?* But, of course, I don't do anything of the sort.

Instead of letting me in so I can revel in Louise's grief, Hilda comes out onto the step and pulls the door to.

"You heard?" she asks in a whisper.

"I did. And about Colin."

Her bottom lip wobbles — such a joy to see — and she blurts, "What about *my* boy?"

"What about him? This is just an unfortunate coincidence, surely. Two men in the wrong place at the wrong time." Hilarity bubbles up my windpipe. I swallow to force it away and compose my face into a suitable mask for this kind of conversation. "Are you worried about Teddy having his head bashed in and all?"

Stupid name for a stupid boy. And he matches his nickname; he's so packed with fat he's undoubtedly as cuddly as a teddy now. Ate too many Burger Kings, that one.

"Of course I am. Will you warn him?" Hilda presses her fingertips to her eyes and rubs in circular motions.

The squelching noise has me seeing red.

A tear dribbles down her cheek. Hilda, crying? Well, now, that's as turn up. She's usually hard-hearted and more bitter than me, which is amazing, considering what I've been through.

"Why don't *you* warn him?" I suggest. "*You're* his mother." A delightfully low blow, so low it could be in Hell with Alfie.

Hilda drops her hands to her sides, her eyelashes drenched. "You know I can't do that."

"Then warn him as his auntie. That's what they all think we are, don't they?" Or *thought we were*, I should say, in Colin's and Francis' cases. Inner chuckle. "All their lives they've called us that, so why not give Teddy a tinkle and tell him you think he might be next."

"Don't be so ridiculous," Hilda snaps, back to her usual acerbic self.

That word. God, how I hate it.

"Then you don't care about him as much as you'd like us to think, do you." I fight a smirk that wants to spread. Difficult, that.

"But he thinks you're his mum, so wouldn't it sound better coming from you?"

Hilda has that beseeching look about her, like the one she used when she begged me to take her spawn of the Devil in and rear him as my own.

I should have told her to shove her proposal where the sun don't shine.

Hindsight isn't a wonderful thing, it's a spiteful twat.

"No." I sound defiant, angry, and so I should. "There's no love lost between us. If I phone him, he'll think I give a shit, and I never have. I did the basics — fed him, housed him, and made sure he didn't go without material things. I couldn't, however, love him, and you knew I wouldn't from day one, and that makes what you did a hundred times worse, giving him to someone who doesn't care. Anyway, he's moving to Scotland soon."

"What?" Hilda pales and darts her eyes left and right, as though fearing someone will hear our conversation. Seems she's still stuck in the past as much as I am, worrying about things people in this day and age couldn't give a fiddler's fuck about.

"I *said* he's moving to Scotland soon."

"I heard you, I just . . ." Panic contracts her face into a grimace. "Have you told him something you shouldn't?"

"What, that William is the father he should have had, and you gave him to me as soon as your old man got confirmation you'd been playing away? No, I didn't tell him that, but you have no idea how many times I've been tempted." Below the belt again, and I wonder if there's anything beneath Hell. If there is, that's where my jibe has gone.

"So he's not going there to find William then?"

"Of course he bloody well isn't. Get out of my way so I can go and see Louise."

I stopped calling her Lou years ago.

You only call people you like by their nicknames.

I nudge her to one side with my weapon, resisting the urge to use it on her head, telling myself I can do that soon enough when I catch up with Teddy the Fast-Food Muncher tonight. He goes to darts the same evening every week, finishes about nine, so that gives me the pleasure of watching one of my soaps before I go to the Orange Pebble in time for him to come bumbling out.

Inside Louise's is much the same as it was in the eighties. She hasn't kept up with the changing interior fashions, and her carpet is worn and in need of ripping up. I'm surprised darling Francis didn't buy a new one for her and pay for it to be laid, seeing as he was such a good, caring son.

I move into the living room, and the childless bitch is sitting on her sofa, quietly staring into space. She must have finished with the noisy sobbing already.

"Hello," I say and sit in the chair opposite so I can see her better. See every ounce of her agony. "I thought it best I pop round."

"To what, gloat that Teddy is still alive?" She turns her eyes into slits and cuffs her nose with the sleeve of her cardigan.

Dirty tart.

"Not to gloat, no, but it is interesting how fate has stepped in to right the wrongs, don't you think?" I'm getting better at these barbs. "Shame it took so long, but sometimes that lovely lady called Karma takes her time. She's probably so busy, after all, what with the way people treat each other. The way actions from others make someone behave in ways they wouldn't have dreamt before they'd been treated poorly."

Louise opens her mouth as if to say something, but Hilda barges in and stands beside my seat, staring down as though I'm supposed to be afraid of her.

That's a laugh.

"You're despicable," Hilda says, "talking to our Lou like that."

"*Our* Lou?" I chuckle. "She might be yours, but she certainly isn't mine." I clutch my weapon, willing myself not to launch it at the pair of them. The only reason I manage it is because I want them living in torment, not at peace in their graves. They don't deserve that. "Shame your Lionel isn't here to help you through your grief, isn't it, Louise?" It isn't, but it's the kind of comment that will put another knife in her heart. "Then again, he'd be mourning the loss of a son that wasn't his, wouldn't he." I pause to let that sink in. Let them know I haven't forgotten, that I'll *never* forget. "Terrible to lose something you once held so dear, too, don't you reckon?"

Like hopes and dreams, trust, and thinking you'll have a devoted husband and plenty of children, only for that husband you vowed to cherish all your life to have sex with the friends who professed to love you like a sister, and everything goes down the shitter.

"Get out," Lou says. "Just get out."

"You never did say sorry to me," I say. "Either of you." I stand and walk to the door, leaning on my weapon, even though it's just been a prop for years to give the impression I'm frail and weak. *Frail and weak my arse.* "Still, you'll be sorry now, I suspect. Have fun battling through the anguish, won't you. I can tell you from experience it's a hard slog."

"You're a wicked cow," Hilda pipes up.

"Takes one to know one." I smile at her. "Maybe one day you'll be sorry, too, just like *our* Lou and Beryl."

I leave then, stepping outside to breathe air that isn't tainted by the likes of those two, down the step, onto the path, then out of the garden and along the way to my house.

Oh, for . . .

He's standing there, as wide as a house and just as tall, and I steam past him, into my sanctuary, leaving the door open for him to follow.

"I came to see if you were okay." He shuts the door and lumbers into the kitchen.

Again? What's with the concern all of a sudden?

"I'm fine." Sodding ecstatic, actually. "What do you want to see if I'm okay about *now*?"

"Well, I got the news about Francis and Colin. Why didn't you tell me about Colin when I was here last night?"

"Didn't realise I needed to." Kettle filled, I stick it on its base and flick the switch to boil. Take out one cup — he won't be staying long enough to drink one — and add tea leaves to the pot.

"But they were like my brothers, so *of course* you needed to."

I bite my tongue.

Hard.

He sinks down onto a chair, props his elbows on the table, and holds his head in his hands. I study him and may well need to use extra force when it's his turn to go on his final shuffle. He's taller than the other two, and with the weight he's carrying, he might well manage to knock me flying if I don't hit him hard enough the first time.

"I don't need to do anything I don't want to do, not anymore." The kettle has boiled — I only ever put enough in it for one or two cups — so I half fill the pot with water and stick the cosy on top. "Are you going to Scotland for any particular reason?"

"Work. I told you it was for work." He lifts his head and slaps his hands on the table. "How can you change the subject like that when Colin and Francis have been murdered?"

Murdered? No, shit for brains, they were given their just desserts, they weren't murdered.

"I didn't take to those boys, so why should I be upset when I didn't like them? Death doesn't make anyone a better person. If they were arseholes in life, they're still the same in death."

"Let's be honest, you've never liked me either, have you?"

I chortle inwardly that he's at last had the balls to say something about that. "No. Glad you noticed."

"Mum, what's *wrong* with you? Other mums don't treat their kids the way you've treated me."

Don't. Call. Me. Mum.

"For a forty-one-year-old, you don't half sound childish." I pour my tea.

"Why did you want to know about Scotland?" he asks, drawing circles on the table with a fingertip.

That's miffed me. I've not long polished that. "Stop doing that, you brat."

He whips his hands down onto his lap beneath the table.

"Got into bad habits since you left home, I see." Milk and sugar in my cup will make for a nice brew. I sip. Yes, lovely.

"No, not at all." He stands, and for the first time his height seems imposing, threatening instead of just a soft and kindly marshmallow man. "I'm actually allowed to breathe at home, unlike when I was a kid. I'm allowed to be me — I can speak and sing and all sorts. Amazing that. It's what proper people do. They live. They're happy — or they try to be when they've got a past they'd rather forget. I don't think I've seen you smile. Ever. You're a nasty, mean old bitch, and I've had enough of your acerbic tongue to last a lifetime."

Acerbic, acerbic, acerbic . . .

"Get out," I say, reminding myself of Louise. "Get out before I chuck this tea in your face."

“Wouldn’t be the first time, would it.” He steps to the kitchen door. “I’m going, and don’t expect to ever see me again.”

Oh, I’ll be seeing you again all right.

He leaves, and a great rush of relief sweeps through me that it’s nearly over. It’s going to come to an end, and I can hardly wait to see what eight o’clock brings.

First, though, I’m going to nip to the hospital to see Beryl.

* * *

The air stinks of piss, disinfectant, and old lady perfume, maybe a hint of Brut and Old Spice from the bloke section across the corridor. The NHS has gone to shit, and the place has a tired feel to it. Scuff marks on the walls, worn lino down the centre of the floor, faded curtains.

Or maybe that’s just this ward, where old people have come to die. Not like they’re bothered about the decor, is it.

Sobering.

Beside the window, Beryl’s in bed, the three others surprisingly empty. Maybe the occupants popped their clogs overnight and no one else is at death’s door yet or ill enough to fill them. Doesn’t ring true with what I’ve heard on the news. Shortage of beds this, people on trolleys in corridors that.

Comes a time in your life when you realise almost everything is based on a lie.

Beryl stares over, and she’s lucid, a wan smile appearing. Hilda bullshitted me then. Beryl isn’t fighting for her life at all. All right, she’s pale, her skin grey and wrinkled, but she’s hardly going to kark it any time soon.

I sit beside her bed, and she takes my hand. Hers is spindly and light, the bones sticking up beneath the skin, so different to mine that I’m thinking she might be wasting away after all.

“How are you?” I ask, wondering whether I should tell her about Francis to help her on her way to the pearly gates.

Despite her being the better friend out of the three, she still deceived me. Still hurt me.

"I should be okay to go home tomorrow," she says. "Not that I want to. I prayed last night I wouldn't wake up. I didn't want to face life without . . ." A tear trickles down her cheek.

I love the sight of it. If I could bottle it to look at every so often, I would.

"There's something I need to tell you." She squeezes my hand as much as she's able.

"Oh right. What's that then?" Has this brush with death given her a conscience?

Years ago, she'd said, "It isn't how you think. At least not in my case."

I'd asked her what she'd meant, but she hadn't elaborated. Said she needed to forget about it, otherwise life wouldn't be worth living.

Then she'd said, "Please know I would never deliberately hurt you."

Cryptic. But she *had* hurt me by having Colin.

Now, she looks at me, her eyes watery, and says, "Alfie raped me that night."

I can't breathe. The walls are closing in, and my mind goes blank. Then survival instinct kicks in, like it has so many times in the past, and I straighten my spine, take a deep breath. This has changed everything. Colin . . . I killed Colin, and all the while . . .

No, she still chose to have him.

"Tell me what happened."

"He . . . we were in the hotel in a room reserved for the party." Her eyelids flutter. "Then Alfie said he had something to show us — me, Hilda, and Louise. We went up in a lift, and he took us to a room. He must have reserved it."

So he'd planned what he was going to do.

I close my eyes, unsure whether I want all the sordid details or not, even though I asked her to tell me. I've imagined the scenario a million times, tormenting myself, seeing how he touched them, how they touched him, but never, never did I see him taking Beryl against her will.

The scratches on his back. His cheek.

"I believe you," I say. "I . . ."

"It started by him flirting, and the other two, they were so drunk. He came on to them, and they . . . they did what they did, and I sat on a chair in the corner with my eyes shut, wishing I had the courage to leave, but I thought if I did, I'd lose my job, and we weren't in the best of situations with money back then, and I—"

"Do the other two know what he did to you?" My heart hurts.

She shakes her head. "They left after . . . well, after, and he told me to stay where I was. Then he . . . And later, when we all found out we were pregnant, I lied and told them I did it with him willingly."

Something has bothered me all these years, so I ask, "Your husbands. Always wore condoms. How did you get around that? Say they'd split?"

She nodded.

"Bit of a coincidence it happened to all three of you." I take my hand from hers. Rub my forehead, my fingertips cold. "But they all swallowed it apart from William."

Beryl squeezes her eyes closed for a moment. "You should never have had to . . ."

"I know. I hated bringing up that boy. Do you understand how I could hate him? How I couldn't stand the sight of him?"

"It was a wicked thing to expect you to do, but if you think back to how it was, the stigma of being a single parent, the way people looked at you if you put a step wrong. That's why I kept my mouth shut about what Alfie had done to me. Do *you* understand how I could?"

"I do." I'm so glad I encouraged that man to die, but I should have done it sooner. Why had I tormented myself living with him all that time to make his life hell? Why hadn't I moved on, left the child behind and started again? Because, like Beryl had said, it was different in those days, but in these more liberal times, I would have packed my bags, and Alfie wouldn't have seen me for dust.

There's nothing I can do about it now. About Colin. If I'd known . . .

But there's still *him* to deal with. *His* mother went with Alfie willingly, as did Francis'.

And there's still a price they must pay for it.

"I kept Colin because . . . I'm a catholic, you know that. It was sin enough to use condoms, but to abort a life? I couldn't do that." Another tear trickles.

I don't want to bottle that one.

Enough. There's too much emotion here now. I have to remain focused. Can't let feelings get in the way.

I rise, patting Beryl's hand. "I'll keep it quiet. From the other two, I mean. I . . . I doubt very much I'll ever speak to them again. Not after today. I went to see them because . . . It didn't go well." It's best I leave the Francis news for when she comes out of hospital. It's Louise's story to tell, not mine. "I'm sorry. About Colin." And it's funny, because I am. I really am.

Deceit led to me thinking the wrong thing, and Colin got caught in my crosshairs when I should never have had my sights on him at all.

Life is so, so unfair.

I leave, letting anger fire my gut, thinking of Alfie doing such a despicable thing to Beryl then continuing as though he didn't do her wrong. Going to parties where she was present, for fuck's sake.

What kind of monster did I marry?

What kind of monster did he make me?

I wish he were alive so I could kill that son of a bitch all over again.

CHAPTER TWENTY

The second dog walker didn't have anything to say that would help the case. He'd crossed the football pitch, thrown a ball for the dog, and the mutt had bounded into the woods to get it. There was the body, and Bob's your uncle.

At a corner table in Costa by the window, Tracy wrapped her hands around her tall cup, and memories of another time in a café flitted into her mind. There, she'd had her first encounter with Dr Schumer, although she'd referred to him as Dr F (Dr Fuckface). She wondered whether he would have fixed her as he'd promised if he hadn't died, then told herself no one could fix her, not even Damon.

Or herself.

She'd always be a broken bird.

She wasn't broken enough not to do her best on the job, though. It fired her blood, the need to catch criminals, and she doubted it would ever leave her.

Damon sat opposite, and her thoughts switched to him and how he'd had to take months off work after Lisa had stabbed him. To recuperate — and decide whether policing was still the career for him. She wondered how he'd take it if he found out the woman who had jabbed a knife into him was her sister and not her father's lover like Tracy had led everyone to believe. Damon had chatted about both of them giving their careers up, doing something else entirely, but Tracy had known she'd never do that. Then the squad job had come up, and Winter had contacted her personally, and together, she and Damon had agreed to give it another shot, working side by side to right the wrongs and get some sense of peace in their lives.

It had worked until her sister had reappeared.

Should she tell Damon the truth now or keep it hidden forever?

"You've gone inside your head," he said, picking at a cheese twist that was burnt at the edges.

"It happens. I'm trying to fathom everything. To know the best route to take." She wasn't lying, so that was something.

"About what?"

Fuck. *Now* she'd have to lie. "The case. You know, what might have gone on between Beryl Spinks and Louise Vale. Something must have. Especially if we don't find a sinister connection between Colin and Francis."

"Hmm."

People walked by outside in her peripheral vision, and she sipped her coffee, savouring the short break they were having. Once they returned to the station, it would be all systems go, or maybe the team had found the link already. Then again, Nada would have contacted her if that were the case.

Someone stopped right beside the window, and Tracy flicked her attention in that direction, ready to give the person a filthy look for encroaching on their personal space, albeit from outside. A piece of glass was only so thick, and the barrier didn't take away the transparency.

It didn't take away the appearance of Lisa, either, staring inside, appearing as though she'd donated her brain to science before she was done with it.

"What the *fuck*!" Damon's cup crashed over, and the cheese twist went flying. He rose, glaring at Lisa, walking backwards, no doubt to keep his focus on her while he left the shop.

Tracy's heartbeat went haywire, thrumming up a storm, and for a second or two she couldn't move. This was it. This was where everything came tumbling down and her treachery would be highlighted with a winking neon sign: DAMON, YOUR GIRLFRIEND IS A FIRST-CLASS LIAR.

Then she regained the use of her limbs, her brain, and shot up, pleading with her eyes for Lisa to get the hell out of here and never come back. What did she *want*? Hadn't Tracy made it clear enough before to not show her fucking face again?

Lisa stared at her, eyes glistening.

I don't need your emotional blackmail. Don't you dare do this to me.

Lisa glanced towards the door, then she ran, scooting across the road, a four-deep crowd outside the cinema engulfing her. Damon raced after her, dodging a car that was going too fast and would have hit him if he hadn't been fast enough, and he, too, disappeared inside the throng.

Tracy left Costa, her legs weak, her stomach hollow, and gave chase. She elbowed through the waiting moviegoers, into the cinema. Lisa and Damon were nowhere in sight, so she jogged up to the bloke on the refreshment counter and whipped out her ID.

"Did a woman come in here, black hair, grey hoodie, dark-blue jeans, red scarf?"

"No one's been in. Folks round here know they have to wait outside until half an hour before the films start." He stared at her pointedly for breaking the cardinal rule.

She mentally gave him the middle finger.

"I see." She thanked him and left, muscling her way between people packed together as though joined at the damn hip.

On the path, she paced up and down, scanning the area, trying to work out where they'd gone. A glass-fronted shopping centre stood beside the cinema, and she went inside, assaulted by the scents of the standalone perfume booth ahead and a doughnut shop to the right. She took her phone out and dialled Damon, praying like fuck he hadn't caught up with Lisa. If he had, it was game over — and she was screwed six ways to Sunday.

But there he was, walking towards her, his face a mask of anger — and fear if she read the expression right. He looked like he did when things weren't going their way at work, and she sighed in relief that he hadn't found her sister.

"What the hell was *that* all about?" she asked, sliding her phone away.

He stopped in front of her. "Didn't you see her?"

"What, some woman who seemed off her tits on drugs? Yes, I saw her."

"It wasn't just some woman, Trace." He gazed at her meaningfully.

She wasn't about to take the bait. She'd act as sharp as a pound of raw liver if she had to — no way was she going to admit to seeing *her*. "Are you being divvy on purpose?" she asked. "Because that woman was some drug user. Why the hell would you take it into your head to follow her?"

"It was the woman who stabbed me," he all but snarled.

Taken aback by his venomous attitude — although now she came to think of it, if their roles were reversed, *she'd* be pissed off if she saw the person who'd stabbed *her*, too — she said, "Um . . . no, love. That wasn't the same woman I saw — the one who killed John." *But I killed John. Oh God, this is such a nasty web I'm continuing to weave.*

She knew now that Damon could never find out Lisa hadn't been the one to slice the chief's throat. That Tracy had encouraged her to run.

"I swear to you, Trace, it was her."

"The one I know had different coloured hair, and she definitely hadn't looked like *that.* She seemed ill, the one outside Costa. Maybe it was a doppelgänger — or your mind is playing tricks on you." *That's far enough. Gaslighting isn't something I'm a fan of. Stop now. Stop.*

Damon frowned. "I'd love to agree with you, but I don't. It was her. I'll never forget those eyes." He shrugged. "Nothing we can do now but keep watching out for her."

"True. She's long gone." *And hopefully she'll stay gone.* "Let's nip in to see that man — can't remember his name — in the dry cleaners, see if he's thought of anything else since we last saw him."

"Wes Farthing, doesn't have wheels—"

"But he does have legs and a penny. Yeah, yeah, I should have remembered."

She led the way across the street and into Spinks' shop. Wes was there, and surprisingly, so was Natasha Moss.

"Hi," Tracy said. "How are things?"

Natasha's eyes scrunched shut, but Wes smiled.

"Not too bad, considering," Wes said. "And I'm glad you nipped in, because something came up last night." He gave Natasha the side-eye. "Might be better if we talk in private, like."

"Go for your break early," Natasha said. She sank onto a chair behind the counter and massaged her temples.

Wes rounded the counter and left the shop, waiting outside. Tracy watched him. He took out a vape, sucked on it, then released a cloud of smoke that probably smelt of Eton mess.

"How are things, Natasha?" Tracy asked.

"How do you think they are when your fiancé gets killed?"

"I'm sorry. I just wanted to check. I understand why you're a bit prickly." Tracy held off a sigh. "Have you had a chance to think at all? On whether Colin had any enemies?"

"I've thought of nothing but his loss. He had no enemies. Neither did Francis."

News travelled fast.

"Well, we'll be on our way then."

Grateful to be out of the shop, Tracy stood beside the man who had legs but not wheels and said, "Go ahead."

Wes blew out more vapour. Yes, a cross between Eton mess and strawberry bubblegum. "Now, there might not be anything in it, but last night, I was speaking to my old mum, and she told me something that might be significant, might not. Years ago, Colin's mum had an almighty bust-up with another woman in the Orange Pebble. Mum said this was about forty-odd years ago, mind, so her memory might not be as sharp. But there was some community get-together going on, and Beryl was there with two of her friends — Hilda and Louise — and this other woman came along and accused them of having an affair with her husband. It got a bit heated, and the husband they were meant to have been flashing their lady gardens at stepped in and broke it up. Well, the wife, the one doing the accusing, said something like, 'You'd better love your sons while you can, because you never know when they'll be taken away from you.' Bit weird, that, isn't it? Considering Colin's been murdered and now Francis, so Natasha told me."

Very weird. "Hmm. Thanks for that. Any idea who the woman is?"

"No, but Mum said the husband ran Ace Accountants. Alfie someone. She couldn't recall their surname."

Damon cleared his throat. "That's a huge help, thank you."

"Yes, you've been marvellous," Tracy said. "Right then, we'll be off, if that's all?"

"Yep, that's all. Glad to have helped." Wes stepped back to continue vaping.

Tracy nodded then walked across the road, Damon turning his head this way and that, probably searching for Lisa. She got in the car.

In the passenger seat, Damon said, "That's handy, him mentioning Ace Accountants."

"Hmm. But think about it, whoever that woman was is probably the same age as Beryl and co. No way an older woman would be going around smacking men on the head until they're dead. I mean, really?"

"Best get back to the station and run a check, see if the woman is still alive. Even if it turns out to be nothing, we need to talk to her, find out what that argument was all about."

"Alfie, the husband, is dead. Committed suicide, so we can't ask him." She eased out of the parking space and headed back to work.

Damon browsed his phone. "I tell you, when you start peeling back the layers . . ."

"I know. Cans of worms have nothing on this." *And you really don't want to open the can I've got hidden. It stinks like dishonesty warmed over.*

At the station, she grabbed a vending machine coffee then joined everyone in the incident room. She related what Wes Farthing had told them, then said, "What have you got, Nada?" As far as Tracy was concerned, Nada was in charge while Tracy and Damon weren't around, so she'd field her questions to her.

"Ace Accountants closed after the owner died. He jumped in front of a train a few years ago. Alfie Remmings. Widow, Ivy." Nada bit her bottom lip. "And she lives at twenty-two Robin's Way."

"*What?*" Tracy's stomach bottomed out.

"That's what I thought. So she lives next door to Hilda Jones."

"That street — and that woman — will be the death of me." Tracy rubbed her eyes. "Anything else?"

"I did something that might get my arse kicked," Nada said. "You said we're not allowed to do anything without running it by you first, and I rang you, but you didn't answer."

Tracy took her phone out. She'd missed a call around the time she'd been pursuing Damon when he'd chased after Lisa. Bloody hell. "And . . ."

"So I checked with Winter if it was okay for me to ring Alison Imers, as she went to school with Francis Vale. Alison said Francis and Colin and some other lad all hung around together. She said they acted like brothers, not just friends. Kind of looked like each other, too."

"Did you find out who the other lad is?"

"She couldn't remember his name, so I poked about a bit and looked into Ivy Remmings and whether she has any children — you know, in case we need to warn her and her child — but there's no record of her having given birth anywhere. However . . ." Nada inhaled a huge gulp of air then let it out. "Hilda Jones had a child in the seventies — a fortnight after Colin was born — in a small cottage hospital a few miles away which has since closed down."

"Jesus Christ. That bitch told me she didn't have kids." Fury erupted inside Tracy, and she paced, livid that Jones had lied to her — and for what? Had she given her baby away, was that it? Not unheard of, especially back then, but . . . Okay, Tracy could understand Jones supplying that answer. She *didn't* have a child if she'd put it up for foster or adoption. "I'm going to have to visit this Ivy Remmings. Hmm. Did you check the education system, see if any kids called Remmings appeared?"

"No, I didn't. I'll do that now." Nada swivelled her chair to face her desk. "Might take me a while."

"I appreciate that. Actually, to make it easier and cut down on time, ring Alison Imers back, see what school they all went to." Tracy smiled at the others. "Alistair, did you find anything we might have missed?"

"No, boss. I came to the same conclusion as you all did — there was nothing up to the point the new information came in, when I came on board."

"Phew. Means we're not losing our touch. Fine. Lara, Erica, Tim?"

They shook their heads.

"Well then, I'm going with Damon to Remmings'. Keep poking around — mainly into the Remmings — both of them — and this kid who happens to be a damn ghost. He's got to be in the system somewhere if he went to school. We need to warn him and his mother he could be in danger."

CHAPTER TWENTY-ONE

That detective is at my front door. The man is with her, too. She's banging on it like no one's business, and I'm not sure what to do, standing here on the other side of the street beside a wheelie bin. I could join them, ask what they want, and play the pitiful old lady, or I could hang around until they piss off.

They can't know it was me. I've been too careful.

I'm going over there.

I hobble, using my weapon for support, and hunch my back to give the impression I'm well past it, likely to drop dead any minute. It's worked wonders in the past.

At my gate, I squint at them standing on my step, and they turn, the woman glaring daggers and the man smiling as if I'm his favourite granny.

Good cop, bad cop.

No one is ever original these days. Sheep, the lot of them.

I sigh and amble up the path, giving a wince or two with every step. "Can I help you?" I want to laugh at my reedy, old-as-God voice but manage to keep it inside. Wouldn't do to be wetting myself in this situation.

"Ivy Remmings?" the woman asks.

"Yes?" I make a show of trying to get my keys out of my handbag, and the man comes down to hold my elbow so I can get them out. What a gent. "Thank you. So kind." I smile at him and pat his arm.

"DI Collier and DS Hanks," she says.

I climb the step and open the door. "Is it about poor Colin and Francis?" Inside, I turn to face them. "So awful." I wobble my bottom lip.

"Mrs Remmings, please could we come in for a moment? I don't want to discuss things outside." Collier cocks her head in the direction of Hilda's.

I get the gist. "Oh. I see. Yes."

I shuffle in, hanging my coat on the hook and leaning my weapon against the wall so I can remove my shoes and put on my slippers. Then I take my crutch and go into the kitchen. "Come on then. I'll make us some tea. I imagine you don't get many chances to have a cuppa at work."

They follow me in and take a seat at the table without being asked. People of today, they have no manners. With the kettle on and the teapot in place on the worktop, I stay beside the sink and wait, my back so bowed my nose will be touching the damn tap in a minute.

"I haven't got much time," Collier says, "so don't worry about tea for us. I'll get straight to it. Do you have a son?"

I shake my head. "Sadly, that wasn't something I was blessed with. I've never given birth." *I'm not lying, just bending perceptions a bit. Oh God, will she go and ask the neighbours about him?*

"Do you know Mrs Jones well from next door?"

"I used to work with her, ooh, many years ago now. Yes, I know her well. We've lived beside each other for just over four decades."

"Does *she* have a son?"

I throw out a puzzled face. "She's lived there alone for almost the whole time I've been here. Her husband left her in the seventies. She never remarried." *Let Hilda explain that one — William didn't die like she told everyone. He walked out.*

"I see." Collier frowns, and it looks like it might hurt. She'll give herself a headache if she's not careful. "As you've mentioned, you're aware of what happened to Colin and Francis. Did you know them well, too?"

"Of course. If you live somewhere this long, you tend to know many people well. I know their mothers, too. Beryl is one of my closest friends. In fact, I've just got back from visiting her in the hospital. They say she can come home tomorrow."

"Oh, that's wonderful." Collier's face transforms into an expression of relief mixed with happiness. She's much more attractive when she isn't scowling.

I sense a kindred spirit in her. Someone with a past she'd rather forget. When you've been through the wars, you tend to pick up when someone else has fought the good fight, too. An invisible thread joins all the used and abused souls, and you can see it if you peer hard enough.

"Do you know of a boy who went to school with Colin and Francis? He may have gone to their homes for tea, played with them." She seems to be on pins and needles.

"Can't say I know of anyone going there for tea. Then again, I don't stay glued to my window, so, you know . . ."

"I understand. Do you know of anyone who might have a grudge against Colin and Francis?"

Haha. Hahaha. "Can't say I do, no."

"Now, it's come to our attention that a good few years ago you had an altercation with Beryl Spinks, Louise Vale, and Hilda Jones in the Orange Pebble. You accused them of having an affair with your husband, Alfie."

Dread swirls in my stomach. How did they find out about that? I curse myself for the hundredth time for ever going into that pub and spouting my mouth off. I should have kept it behind closed doors like Alfie had insisted, but I was young and angry and thought I knew best.

"I did." It won't do to lie this time. "But of course, it was just rumours. They were my friends. They wouldn't have done such a thing. When you're young you see things magnified.

You don't think straight. I stormed in there and made quite a fool of myself." I titter to ram home my stupidity.

"That's not what I'm concerned about," she says, eyeing me, the mouse on her trap, sniffing the cheese.

Be careful.

"What bothers me is what you said about their sons." Collier stares — hard. "Something about loving their sons while they can because they don't know when they'll be taken away from them."

"Ah, that's been skewed, as rumours usually are." More titters. Relief flows through me that I can get out of this sticky situation. The kettle has boiled, so I turn and delve into the task of making the tea. I don't have to see them staring at me then. "As I told you, I haven't been able to have children, and at the time of the argument, it was obvious I'd never have them. Time had passed, and I'd never fallen pregnant. I wanted them to appreciate their boys, and me mentioning the taken away from them bit — well, that was my way of trying to say my ability to have children was taken away, do you understand?"

"I think so," she says, giving me a somewhat sad smile.

I've won her over.

Ivy, you should have been an actress.

Collier rises and comes over to me, standing there with sorrow in her eyes, and I don't think I can take the pity, so I turn away and spoon sugar into my cup, deliberately shaking my hand so some grains spill on the worktop.

"It's a terrible thing, getting old," I say and wipe up the spill. "I must go to the doctor about these tremors."

"You do that." She rests a hand on my shoulder. "If you think of anything significant, will you call me?"

Not on your bleedin' life.

She places a card beside my teapot then leaves, the man going with her.

I stare through the nets at the window.

She's going round to Hilda's.

Shit. *Shit.*

CHAPTER TWENTY-TWO

Hilda Jones stood in the doorway, meaty hands on hips, her Trunchbull face twisted in a snarl. "What do you bloody want *now*?"

Not giving her the same courtesy as Ivy Remmings and asking to go inside, Tracy said, "You had a son in nineteen seventy-seven."

Jones staggered against the doorframe, squashing her arm. "What?"

"I don't think you need me to repeat what I just said." This woman had Tracy wanting to upset her, but she had to remain professional. For the most part. "Where is he?"

"I-I don't know." Hilda's face flushed, her pulse throbbing so hard the baggy skin at her neck wobbled. "Who told you?"

"We found out during the course of our investigation. Did you think we wouldn't? You do realise we could have you for perverting the course of justice, don't you." Scaring the woman might be going a little too far, but Tracy didn't give a stuff at the moment. Maybe she'd feel guilty later down the line, but . . .

"So Ivy next door told you, did she?" Jones paled then, her eyes watering.

"No, she didn't. What happened to him?" Tracy asked.

"He was adopted."

"I see. Fine. We'll look into records and find him ourselves. What with Mr Spinks and Mr Vale dying . . ."

Hilda stumbled backwards, and Damon leapt inside to steady her.

"Are you all right?" he asked, one arm around her back, a hand on her elbow.

"Yes, yes. I just didn't expect my past to come back like this, that's all."

Don't we all . . .

Jones didn't seem so blustery now, all the wind knocked out of her previously billowing sails.

Tracy almost muttered *good* but held it at bay. The past coming back wasn't the best of things, Tracy knew that better than anyone. A sliver of guilt pinched her heart — *damn it* — but she swept it away. Getting sentimental wouldn't help this case.

"Damon," she said and walked down the path and to the car.

He never said a word on the way back to the station, and she was glad. It wasn't always constructive to have someone wittering on in your earhole, was it. Sometimes it was better to talk to yourself. You didn't feel you couldn't say 'fuck off' or 'mind your own business' then.

So, Ivy Remmings hadn't had any children. Hilda Jones had a son. Perhaps they could interview Louise Vale and Beryl Spinks again tomorrow — give them some space for now to digest the loss of their boys. Tracy doubted Jones' lad would be in danger — after all, he'd probably been adopted in another county so he didn't bump into his real mother. If no one was aware Jones had a kid, there was no one to go after him, was there?

In the incident room, she gave everyone an update. They gave theirs — nothing.

"Why haven't you got anything about the lad who hung around with Colin and Francis? Surely he's in some sort of database, and then there's the school itself. Nada?"

"Sod's law, boss, but the computers are down — the ones we need to access for education records. Something to do with the server." Nada grimaced. "I rang the school, and there aren't any tangible files around, not for that far back — they've been transferred into digital, and they can't access the database either."

"Fuck. So with no access at the moment, we can't do anything but wait. Unless I go and visit Mrs Spinks in hospital and give Mrs Vale a bell." She scratched behind her ear. "Okay, I'll do that, you all continue searching — for anything, you hear me? Have a poke about on their Facebooks — they *must* have friends in common. I don't get why Francis and Colin weren't friends on social media. Something to look into?"

They nodded, and she crooked a finger for Damon to follow her.

In her office, she closed the door behind him. "Can you ring Louise Vale for me? No way is she going to want to talk to me."

He nodded. Tracy left the room to get them a hot drink. Five minutes to chill was needed, otherwise she was going to self-combust. Frustration built inside, and while she waited for the crappy vending coffee to spurt into the thin plastic cups that let too much heat through and burnt your fingers, she took a moment to input the link Winter had given her into her phone. She ordered coffee beans, the creamer, and a machine for use in the incident room. No one here deserved to drink this crap.

She took the drinks to her office and closed the door with the side of her foot. Fingertips boiling, she placed the cups on the desk.

"Well?" she asked.

"She said she doesn't know who he hung around with at school."

"Christ. Anything else?"

"And that she didn't feel up to talking."

"Understandable. Listen, I don't fancy trekking all the way to the hospital to talk to Beryl. I feel bad enough she had a heart attack in the first place. Who knows whether she'll shit herself again if I waltz in there." She lifted the phone and pressed the number for Nada's desk. "Hey, it's me. Ring the hospital — Horley General, isn't it? — and get a nurse to ask Beryl Spinks whether she remembers who Colin went to school with. I don't think it's advisable I do it."

"All right, boss. Get back with you in a sec."

"Thanks."

Tracy sat in the spare chair, seeing as Damon was in her seat having phoned Louise Vale. She let out a long breath and closed her eyes, relaxing her muscles. Tension dissipated, and she peeked through half-mast lids at Damon, who appeared away with the fairies.

"You all right?" she asked.

"Yeah. Just been a weird day, that's all."

Lisa.

"It has. You know, I just don't get what's going on. Did you believe Ivy Remmings?" She threaded a hand through her hair, some of it snagging on a knuckle.

"She seemed genuine enough. Although she's tall and built, she still looked frail somehow. I can't see her being able to kill anyone, can you? I mean, she's got a curved spine, for God's sake. And she can't walk without that crutch."

"True. Unsteady hands, too. Shaking. So Farthing's info about her is probably just something we can put to one side. Shit." She got up to get her coffee, but her desk phone rang. "Hello?"

"Nada, boss."

"Yep."

"About Beryl Spinks . . ."

"Uh-huh."

"Um, she's dead."

* * *

The Past

"Mum, can I go and play with Col and Francis?"

If he asks me that again, I'm likely to slap the little sod. Since he's been going to school, he's out from under my control for six hours a day.

I should have kept him at home and taught him myself. When Alfie had told me to enrol him, using that fake birth certificate, I had almost lost it. Why did it have to be me? Why couldn't he do it?

"No. You get to play with them at school and on a Tuesday after. That's enough."

The weekly meetings between us all still go on, just that we do it when school has finished instead. The children enjoy a game of football in my back garden, and Hilda, playing the doting aunt, takes care of him if he needs anything so I don't have to.

Suits me.

In the end, I'd given in about him going to school so I didn't have to see his ugly mug so much. I'd asked Alfie if I could go back to work while he *wasn't around, but he'd said no. He prefers me at home — I suspect he's needing the comfort of his latest secretary more than ever, as I haven't let him touch me since I found out he had three children on the way.*

We live a lie, all of us.

The child pouts at me. He knows better than to do that. I open my mouth to tell him off, but a knock at the door means I have to leave him standing there by the kitchen sink looking as though Father Christmas didn't deliver him any gifts.

He wouldn't if I had my way.

I open the door. Louise stands there, her face streaked with tears, cheeks red.

"Oh my God," she says. "I . . . I . . ."

Something is clearly wrong. I know what it is, I just want her to say it. "Get in here." I grab her arm and haul her inside, close the door, then yank her into the kitchen.

It feels good to manhandle her.

The child stares at 'Auntie' Lou, clearly upset that she's *upset.*

"Go upstairs," I snap at him.

He doesn't argue — knows better, that one — and bolts away.

"Sit." I press Louise into a chair at the table. "What the hell is wrong with you now?"

There's always something going on at her house. Either Lionel is causing trouble with his drinking then shouting at her when he comes home, or she's wailing, hysterical about it. A never-ending saga is the life of Louise Vale. She used to think it was cute that their names started with the same letter. Said it was meant to be. A few months ago she said she wished she'd never met him.

I often wonder whether he knows what happened and took to the drink to blot it out.

"He's . . . he's dead." She sobs.

The sound of her crying has me wanting to slap her. "Who's dead?"

"Lionel!" The word comes out elongated, high-pitched, and is worthy of me kicking her in the head for even uttering it in that way.

"Excuse me?" I'm the concerned friend and neighbour, the one who will be there for her in her hour of need. Or a few minutes anyway, as I can't cope with her for longer than that. "That's . . . that's awful. How did it happen?"

"The p-p-police said he'd fallen into the canal this morning."

"Oh my . . ." Fallen. Ha ha. "How tragic. What was he doing there?"

"He was on about hiring a barge for a holiday, and he'd gone to the rental place to book it. He made it there, paid the deposit, but he never turned up at work after. He was meant to start at eleven today because the bricks weren't due at the building site he was on until then."

"Will you still go on the holiday?" The insane urge to laugh at my unfeeling question grips me.

"What?"

"Doesn't matter. Can't he swim?" I know full well he can't. Couldn't. He'd thrashed about trying to reach the side then sank beneath the surface, only a few bubbles left right at the end from his last exhalation.

"No," she whispers. "What will I do without him?"

"I thought you were thinking of leaving him anyway. You said his drinking had got too bad. So why are you so upset?"

"I don't know . . ."

"Neither do I." I go into the living room, pour her a stiff one from the drink globe, then return and shove it under her nose. "Neck it. You've had a shock. Where's Francis?" Not that I care.

"He's round at Beryl's with Colin."

Ah, so that's why the little fucker upstairs wanted to play with them.

"Where's Hilda?"

"She went out this afternoon, said she wouldn't be back until tonight."

"Oh, so that's why you're here, is it? You didn't want to go round Beryl's because Francis would see the silly state you've got yourself into, and Hilda isn't there to comfort you. Charming."

She has the grace to blush.

I have no grace and say, "Finish your drink and piss off."

"Ivy!"

"What? You think I enjoy being your last port of call all the time?"

"No."

"No, I don't. Now go and grieve with your other friends, because this one doesn't care."

She stumbles out of the house, twisting her ankle as she goes down the front step. She cries out for my help, but I close the door, pleased with how distraught she is, how she's in pain.

An eye for an eye.

* * *

Two Years Later

Beryl barges into my house emitting a stream of sobs that dances on my almost nonexistent sympathy bone with heavy boots, stomping all the compassion out of me.

"He's . . . he's dead!" she says on a hiccough.

"Who?" I work hard not to smile.

"Norm."

Her husband, an insipid sort with no backbone. A 'yes' man, always doing whatever Beryl says. She adores him, so this turn of events is going to really sting.

Excellent.

"Oh my goodness." I thud into a kitchen chair and rest my hand over my heart. "How?"

She leans against the cupboard closest to the table. "Someone . . . someone . . . put a plastic bag over his head and suff . . . suffocated him."

It had been a tough one. He'd struggled, but as I'm taller than him, stronger — he was a weedy little git — he'd lost the fight faster than Alfie or Lionel would have.

"Oh. Well. That's just dreadful. When did it happen?"

"Lunchtime. He left the dry cleaners to go to the sandwich shop and never made it back."

Norman had opened his business a few years ago, and it was thriving. I wonder if Beryl will take it over now he's gone. It'll give her something to focus on other than moping around mourning.

"It's . . ." She calms herself. Sniffs. "I can't . . . We were soul mates. He was my other half. How will I live without him?"

"I'm sure you'll manage, given time. We all move on when tragedy strikes, don't we." A little jibe there. "Grief passes, life goes on." And if you can't put it behind you, you get revenge.

She frowns at me. "He knew everything," she whispers.

Everything? About . . . ? "He did?"

She nods. "I don't know why I'm telling you this now, seeing as Norm's . . . Norm's only just gone, but . . . It isn't how you think. At least not in my case."

"What do you mean?"

"I told him what had happened, and he said I needed to forget about it, otherwise life wouldn't be worth living."

What the devil does she mean by that?

"Ivy, please know I would never deliberately hurt you. Now Norm's not here, I need you more than ever. The other two . . . they're not . . . good women."

"Neither are you really."

"I am. I promise you I am. One day, maybe I'll tell you everything."

I want to press her, to ask her to elaborate, but she's crying again. Something niggles at me, but I can't grasp what it is. My anger at what my three friends have done boils inside me — always bubbling, always erupting — and I can't let Beryl draw me away from my end goal. I can't allow her to get that close to me again.

"You'd better leave." I purse my lips. "I need some time alone."

I'm a cow for dismissing her, I know that, but sometimes my mind gets too full — of too much information, too much hurt — and it's better if I'm left to my own devices until I can weather the turbulence storming through me.

She nods and leaves, and I stare out of the kitchen window, curious as to where she'll go next. She surprises me by not calling on Hilda or Louise, going inside her own home instead.

Maybe she isn't like those two after all.

But it's too late now. My plans have been made, and I'll stick to them no matter what. Emotions don't come into it. Not the good kind anyway.

I boil the kettle and make tea, sipping the hot brew and thinking back to when I killed Norman. I recall every detail and, satisfied no one saw me down the side of the sandwich shop, whispering to Norman, getting him to go down there with me on the pretence I had something important to tell him, I bask in the glow of a job well done.

The child appears in the kitchen doorway then walks to stand in front of me. "Is Uncle Norm dead?"

He must have been listening from the living room.

"What do they say about people who listen in on conversations they're not invited to participate in?" I ask.

"I don't know."

"They say your ears burn because you're doing something you shouldn't. Did your ears burn?"

No." His eyebrows draw together.

I throw the tea at him, and he screams, dancing on the spot, wailing and snotting all over the place.

"Are they burning now?"

CHAPTER TWENTY-THREE

There was nothing for it but to go home at the end of the shift, shocked and feeling guilty that Mrs Spinks had had another heart attack shortly after Mrs Remmings had left her bedside.

On Facebook, Nada had found several friends in common with Colin and Francis. She'd messaged them from the squad's private Facebook page, and four out of the six had responded. None of the four had been to school with the men and only knew Colin through Francis — friends of his from the social club at the recreation grounds when Colin had joined them once after a match win.

The remaining two hadn't replied, and Nada had taken a punt and looked them up on the electoral roll, contacting them via phone on the off chance they were the same men. As luck would have it, they were. They had worked for Colin at the dry cleaners at some point and met Francis at one of the work Christmas parties Francis had attended with his wife to make up the numbers.

Tracy kicked herself for not getting the previous employees' names sooner. Then she told herself she was human and couldn't think of everything. Still, she was in charge and *should* think of everything. When she had a moment, she'd type up an action sheet that must be adhered to with every case. That way, all tasks would be completed, and she wouldn't have to worry about remembering to do them. Assigning specific jobs to each member of her team when a new case began would mean they were all pulling together to act out their roles without her having to breathe down anyone's neck.

And she wouldn't have to chastise herself for fucking up.

At home now, Tracy tried to switch off. This case was a bitch and a half, so it proved difficult to go from work to leisure mode. There was never any leisure when a job was in full swing, not really, but if she didn't step back and smell the roses — or on this case, the curry Damon was cooking — she'd go off her rocker.

She relaxed on their red sofa, her bare feet on the fluffy grey rug in the centre of the room. Head back, she closed her eyes. The sounds of Damon in the kitchen comforted her, giving her a sense of security she hadn't had when they'd lived separately in the city. They were together in all ways now — except for the secrets she continued to keep. They would always be a barrier between them.

A slight tapping out the front had her springing her eyes open, and she sat upright on the edge, cocking her head to listen. It came again, possibly fingernails against the window, and she stood, her heart pounding, fear weakening her body and sending it cold.

She went out into the hallway, glancing at the kitchen door that stood ajar. Damon whistled to a tune coming out of the radio they had in there, so she eased open the front door and peered outside.

"What the *fuck* are you doing here?" she whispered, the words scraping against her throat.

She put the door on the latch and stepped outside. Lisa stood there, shivering, hugging herself, her navy coat hanging off her skinny frame, blood splatter marring one of her cheeks.

"I need . . . I need some more money," Lisa said, teeth chattering.

"I can't get you any right now." Tracy glanced back at the door to make sure it hadn't swung farther open. "Get down here." She gripped Lisa's shoulder and dragged her along the side of the house. "You've been sodding following me, haven't you." Stupid thing to say. Of course she fucking had.

"I need help." Lisa's eyes glistened.

"Too right you do. And where's that blood from?" Tracy swallowed, dreading the answer. *Was* Lisa the killer? If she was, Tracy really shouldn't let her go this time.

"I . . . I owe someone some money. I . . . uh . . . I borrowed it, and they found out. They punched me."

"So you mean you stole it." Tracy's sigh seemed to gust out for ages.

"No." Lisa screwed her face up. "Sort of. I borrowed it mid-shift at work and was going to do some extra in my own time so I could put it back, but my boss called me in, so I couldn't make the cash up."

"Called you in? What the hell are you doing for a living?"

"Um . . ."

"Out with it."

"Prostitute."

"Oh, fuck me."

"It's all I can do. I told you I had a cash-in-hand job and my boss gave me the bedsit."

"Boss? Pimp, you mean. So what did you need the money for?" Tracy stared at her. "Don't tell me. Drugs."

"I'm sorry . . ."

"You will be. You'll be sorry you started taking them when it messes you up even more than you are already."

"I have to get that money. I'll need to go round some pubs and get a sale or two there if you won't give me some."

"No, I won't. Go home, will you. I mean it now, if you come back here or pull a similar stunt like you did today at Costa, I'll fucking haul you in myself, you got that?"

"I'll tell them what you did."

"You do that. I covered my arse. They think it was you who killed John." Tracy's heart kicked up speed. Why the hell was this happening? Hadn't she endured enough? Would she ever live free from fear, the Past something she could look back on without wanting to chuck her guts up? "If I see you again, I swear I'll arrest you."

"You don't love me, do you?" Lisa asked.

If Tracy said she cared, Lisa might continue coming back. "No. I don't. So piss off." Saying that stung more than Tracy thought it would. "I barely know you, so how can I love you?"

Lisa slouched off down the street, a whip of wind grabbing at her hair and throwing it in all directions. Her red scarf, too. Tracy waited for Lisa to get into a clapped-out Ford and drive off, waited some more until she couldn't see the taillights anymore, then stepped inside, locking and bolting the door. She padded into the living room and sat, unease slithering down her spine.

When would this shit end?

CHAPTER TWENTY-FOUR

I stare through the window of the Orange Pebble. There are people inside having a jolly good time, roaring if a dart hits the right number, booing if it doesn't. Folks lift glasses of beer, the froth bubbly, clinging to the upper half like yeast mixed with water ready to make bread. It reminds me of the days I used to make bread, before the sliced stuff came along.

I move away from the pub. I'm behind a tree in the car park now, back in a far corner, waiting. I left home at eight and arrived here at half past, ready for him to come out at nine.

A massive cheer goes up — someone's won it for a team, then — and anticipation builds inside me. This is the last one — the last one in a long line — and I'll be glad when it's all over. What a bumpy road this has been.

A car turns up, red, rust patches all over, and a woman gets out. She looks as rough as a badger's arse and just as shitty. On the tarmac, she gawps about then heads for the Orange Pebble, swiping at her eyes with the front of her wrist.

A few people leave over the next fifteen minutes, chatting about the match win and how the other team could have tried harder.

Such is the way of life, putting the underdog down.

The number one underdog himself strolls out a while later — at least that's how he sees himself, I bet — and I wait in my hiding place for him to waddle over. He always comes this way so he can walk through the park and use the alley to get into Starling Road. It seems right to do him over by the stream, same as Colin.

He's close, so close, but that woman comes out, the badger's bum, and races after him. I hadn't planned for anyone else to be around, and it throws me off. He presses through a gap in the hedges and will come out on the other side onto one of the lawns at the park. Badger goes in after him, whining about giving him a good price and it'll be worth his while.

I follow.

The field is dark, their silhouettes backlit by a mid-grey sky that by rights feels as though it should give more light but doesn't. It dawns on me it's the clouds, that grey colour, the navy-blue of night peering from behind in patches with stars as decoration.

"Go away, I'm not interested," he says, walking off, hands jammed in his trouser pockets.

"I just need fifty quid." Badger. Chasing him. "Fifty quid will see me right."

"I haven't got fifty quid, and even if I did, I'm still not interested. I've got a wife. What do I need another woman for?"

That hurts. I blink. Shame his father didn't have the same morals.

"A blow job isn't really cheating," she calls.

"Go away, will you?"

Yes, go away. You're messing things up.

I thunder after them, anger biting my nerves, ratcheting up my irritation at this whole sorry state of affairs. I'd had my life all mapped out from the moment Alfie was interested in me, but no matter how many plans you make, sometimes fate has other ideas.

And that bitch well and truly shafted me.

"A hand job then?" Badger asks.

"Look, piss off," he says. "Go home."

"I don't want to. I want you."

Oh, she's getting on my wick.

I up my pace, lift my weapon, and bring it down on her back. She goes down to her knees, a screech coming out of her.

Too noisy.

I hit her again, missing her head, connecting with her shoulder, then *he's* there, saying, "Fucking hell, fucking hell, fucking hell . . ." and "*Mum*?"

"I am *not* your mum."

Wallops, they're so satisfying, and several follow on his head, along with his yells and grunts.

He's on his knees, too, then she falls onto her side, moaning and clutching her shoulder. I concentrate on him, cracking my weapon on the top of his head time and again, all the years of torment coming out, lending me strength, passion, the ability to hit someone so hard they're not likely to survive it.

He falls backwards, twitches, goes still.

"You've been nothing but a bloody little bastard your whole life," I say, out of breath, adrenaline flushing away, leaving me weak. "A waste of space, a useless piece of crap. Now *there's* acerbic for you."

A shout sails over the hedge, and I glance that way, fear turning my pulse into a skittering throb.

Someone is coming.

Someone is going to ruin everything.

The badger hauls herself to her feet. She stands there facing me, and I quickly assess my options. If I run, she'll catch me. Then there's that shouter, coming through the hedge gap now. Indecision has me panicking for the first time in years, and my mind won't give me the answer as to what to do.

She comes close, that badger, and I'm struck frozen, fear weighting my feet, my arms, my mouth, so I can't speak. Can't tell her to fuck off like I want to.

"What's going on?" the shouter calls.

The badger is right in front of me now, reaching into her jacket, and then a hot slice boils my belly, ripping up, down, up, down. My mouth drops open, liquid heat soaking my coat, and while I know what it is, I'm having trouble accepting it.

This shouldn't be the end.

This isn't how it was supposed to be.

"Have you ever been gutted?" she asks.

CHAPTER TWENTY-FIVE

In the marquee, ten o'clock at night, halogens lighting the scene, Tracy stood beside the body of a man in his forties, the blond of his hair only visible at the end of one lock, the rest crimson-soaked. His face, covered by a sheen of blood, reminded her of Colin's features more than Francis'. The top of his head gaped with a two-inch by six-inch hole. Same killer as the others, it had to be.

She sighed. This had to be the son she had been desperate to find — could it be Hilda's?

Damon walked out of the tent.

"I've already seen to the woman," Gilbert said, pointing to a mound beneath a sheet. I'd say she's your killer — had a crutch with her. Blood and whatnot on it. The right shape for the injuries in all three murders. Sodding heavy, it is. Like she's had it filled with lead."

Tracy raised her eyebrows at him. "Wouldn't put it past someone to do that." She thought of Mrs Remmings and her crutch. Could it be her? "Does the woman have a spine issue? As in, is she elderly-elderly, or just elderly and still strong?"

"I'd say the latter. She's of the larger variety — not overweight but what they call big-boned. She's around six-foot, weighs approximately seventeen stone, somewhere around that mark. She's kept herself fit. Age . . . hmm, sixty-nine, seventy?"

"Seventy-one if it's who I'm thinking it is. So in your estimation, based on her stature, someone of that age could kill using a weighted crutch?" Wasn't that stretching the realms of possibility?

"Absolutely. She's in good shape by the look of her, got good muscle tone on her arms and legs — as in, she works out."

"Blimey. Any ID on this man?"

"Yep. A Mr Alfie Edward Remmings."

"What?"

"That's what his birth certificate says." Gilbert picked up a baggie from beside the victim and held it up.

There it was, as plain as the blood on the poor bloke on the ground:

ALFIE EDWARD REMMINGS.
FATHER: ALFIE REMMINGS.
MOTHER: IVY REMMINGS.

"But . . . but Ivy Remmings said she hadn't been able to have any children." Confused, Tracy frowned.

"I'll be able to tell you for definite whether she did or didn't once I've had a good look at her." He went on to explain how he'd do that, then said, "But he lives in Starling Road . . ."

There was close-knit and close-knit. The parents in Robin's Way, the kids in Starling. She wondered why this Alfie Remmings wasn't Facebook friends with Colin and Francis. Was he the type to avoid social media?

"And you know this because?" She stared at the other baggies on the ground. A wallet. iPhone.

"Provisional driving license." Gilbert shrugged. "Seeing his picture gave me a bit of a funny turn, I have to say. A fleshier version of Mr Spinks and Mr Vale."

Tracy shook her head — the damn thing was full, stuffed with questions. "Can I have a look at the woman?"

Gilbert moved along and peeled the sheet back to reveal her face.

Tracy's stomach rolled over. "Fuck."

"Know her?" Gilbert cocked his head.

"Yes. Ivy Remmings."

"Hmm, the supposed mother."

"Yes, the also supposed frail woman with a sodding bent back and the tremors."

"She was having you on."

"I'm aware of that." Tracy gritted her teeth. Stared at Ivy's forehead. Written with blood for ink: HELP ME. What? Had Alfie Remmings written that? "How did she die?"

"I'll show you. It'll speak for itself." He drew the sheet down to her groin.

The marquee spun right along with Tracy's head, the sight of the stomach wound too close to home and a terrifying reminder of the Past and the case she would always been running from. This had Lisa written all over it. Bile rose into Tracy's throat, and she teetered, reaching out to grab Gilbert's arm to steady herself.

"You all right?" Gilbert asked, eyes narrowing, and he wrapped an arm around her.

"Um . . . yes." Her pulse thundered. Was she going to be sick? "I'm . . . I just didn't expect to see *that* is all."

"Nice, like a sharp knife through a rare steak, wouldn't you say?" He chuckled.

Tracy closed her eyes momentarily. When she opened them again, the mess was still there, the innards pulled out, draped down Ivy's sides. A folded red scarf had been placed over Ivy's pelvis.

Lisa's red scarf had flapped in the wind tonight.

Tracy had to get away from the evidence — evidence that her sister had killed again. Evidence that Tracy had fucked up in believing Lisa had only murdered before because she'd been manipulated, forced to do it.

Was it in Lisa's blood now? Would she do it again? And why the hell had she even *been* here with the other two?

'I'll need to go round some pubs and get a sale or two there if you won't give me some.'

Dear God . . .

Tracy thanked Gilbert and walked to the tent opening. He said something, a joke, and laughed, but she tuned him out. This wasn't funny. Lisa was at it again, and Tracy had the awful dilemma of whether to let her remain free or actively seek her out. Get her behind bars where she clearly belonged.

The problem was, she had no idea whether Lisa was going by a new name.

Outside, she stripped off her protective clothing and met Damon over by a gap in the hedges.

"That vehicle there." She pointed to a red dilapidated effort in the car park. "Found out who that belongs to?"

Damon nodded. "Stolen a month ago in the city."

"Bloody hell," she whispered. "And guess what? All this . . . this bollocks. It was Ivy Remmings all along."

"You what?"

While he took off his whites, she explained the woman's fitness, the frailty ruse. "Now we just need to work out why the hell she was doing it. And get this . . ." She told him about the birth certificate. "I mean, what the fuck?"

"I've spoken to the bloke who witnessed it," Damon said. "Sent him home now, but we'll question him again, won't we? He kept well back once the old woman started bashing the male victim, rang the police. Someone else was there — he couldn't see the face because of it being dark, but he said it was a woman. Trace, there's something you should know, love."

He's going to tell me what I already know.

"On you go then." Lucky her, the words came out steady.

"The second killer said something. 'Have you ever been gutted?'" He breathed out, the exhalation shaky. "She's back, you know that, don't you? I *told* you it was her at Costa. I *said*, didn't I? And you said it wasn't."

"Shit. That's all we need. Are you okay?" She reached up and curled a hand over his shoulder.

"Knowing my attacker is in this town instead of the city we left to get away from her? No, not really. But I'm going to catch the bitch and put her inside."

"We will. We'll find her eventually." *Lisa, please, just leave. Go the hell away.* "What should we do next?" She wanted to see where his mind was at.

"Should we go and interview the other two women again?"

"What, the Robin's Way duo?"

"Yep."

Relieved he'd gone back to the present case before Lisa had muddled with it, Tracy scratched the back of her head. "Hmm. Jones is the best bet. Louise will still be in a bit of a state, no doubt."

They headed there, Tracy grateful for the heat in the car. She hadn't expected to be called out tonight by Winter. No sooner had the last spoonful of curry gone into her mouth, he'd called. They hadn't yet started on the wine, but she'd be indulging once they got home.

In Robin's Way, she parked outside Jones' and killed the engine. The kitchen light blazed — or she assumed it was the kitchen, thinking the house had the same layout as Ivy's — and the silhouette of the occupant moved from one side of the room to the other.

"Want me to deal with her?" Damon asked.

"Nope. I'll do it."

On Jones' front step, Tracy rapped with her knuckles and waited. The hallway light switched on, and Jones' shadow loomed behind the patterned glass. She opened the door and stared at them, mouth sagging.

"What the hell are you two doing here at this time of night?" she snapped. "I was just off up to bed."

"Please may we come in?" Tracy asked.

"No. I'm in the same camp as Louise. You can bloody well stay out here."

"All right. Have it your way. Do you know an Alfie Remmings?"

A micro-expression — an almost imperceptible flicker beside her right eye. "You know I sodding do. I told you, he killed himself. He was my boss years ago. The Ace Accountants bloke."

"Not *that* Alfie Remmings, Mrs Jones."

The woman's face paled, and she flapped her gums, no words coming out.

"May we come in *now*?" Tracy smiled tightly.

Jones stepped back, tripping on the edge of a carpet runner, then righted herself by leaning on the wall. Tracy and Damon entered, and Tracy walked into the kitchen while Damon guided Jones to a wooden bistro table and chairs. He pressed her into a seat and sat beside her.

"What's happened?" Jones' eyes watered. Tears gave a solemn promise to spill over, and her lower lip quivered.

"Who is the second Alfie Remmings?" Tracy asked, pressing her arse against a cupboard. A door handle jabbed one cheek, so she slid over.

"What's . . . is he all right?" Jones raised a doubled fist to her chin, elbows on the table.

Tracy folded her arms. "Like I said, who is he? *Whose* is he?"

"He's . . . he's . . ." She stared at the ceiling. Contemplating what to say? "Ivy's son."

"You know we can prove that these days, don't you." Giving her an out. The chance to tell the truth. "DNA, and the fact we can see from Ivy's pelvis whether she was ever pregnant. The bones will have separated. Then there are parturition pits if she gave birth vaginally . . ." *Good old Gilbert.*

Jones blinked several times. "I . . ."

"Ivy is dead." Tracy stared hard at her.

"W-what?" The tears dribbled free.

"She was stabbed in the stomach. Is that something Alfie Remmings is likely to have done to his own mother? And as for the fact there isn't a registered birth with Ivy or the original Alfie as parents . . . Throws up lots of questions, don't you think?"

"Who . . ." Jones swiped at her wet face. "Alfie wouldn't have done that. Not my boy."

"*Your* boy, Mrs Jones?"

The woman blushed. "Ivy . . . She was wicked to him. She . . . Oh God. Where's my Alfie?"

"Currently lying next to Ivy in a field at the park. Beaten to death like Colin and Francis."

"Dear God, no. Ivy hated those boys, but . . . I can't see her doing this." She swallowed, the saliva audibly clicking.

"I think you have some explaining to do, don't you?" Tracy cocked her head and waited.

* * *

Jones had provided a spare key and, close to midnight, Tracy, Damon, and the rest of the team, hauled out of their beds by her phone calls, went through Ivy's house. Drawers were rummaged in, cupboards inspected, mattresses lifted. What Tracy expected them to find she didn't know, but there had to be something there that would make sense of this hideous bullshit.

In the living room, Damon helped Tracy to shift the sofa. With nothing underneath, not even a speck of dust, they moved to a wingback chair on four-inch wooden legs. A thick black notebook sat beside a blue biro. Tracy picked the book up, her glove tightening over her knuckles. She opened it at the beginning and almost brought up her dinner.

> *There's only so much you can take, isn't there? I found out tonight that Alfie has had sex with Beryl, Hilda, and Louise, and every single one of them . . . well . . . They're pregnant. It happened on the same night, at the work party in the hotel. I don't know what to do because they're keeping the babies. Why is this happening to me? What did I ever do to deserve this?*

Tracy took a moment to digest the words. Could she find it inside herself to have pity for Ivy? The woman had been through so much, according to Hilda, and the events of the past had clearly sent her off the rails. Would Tracy have gone the same way had she not joined the police force? If she hadn't had a focus to anchor her?

Don't think about that.

She flipped a few pages along.

> *They are all without husbands now. William has left Hilda. Lionel drowned — Louise ought to be grateful she doesn't have to put up with his drunken arse anymore. And Norman . . . he was suffocated, and now Beryl has no one except her shitty little son. Who on earth could kill their friends' husbands? I wonder . . .*

Reading between the lines . . . Damn. This was a vendetta beyond anything Tracy could have imagined. She turned to the last page.

> *Alfie ought to rot in Hell for what he did to Beryl. She told me today he raped her that night, and Norman stood by her, knowingly bringing Colin up as his own. Why couldn't I have married a man like that? Why was I the one with a man who couldn't keep his hands and cock to himself? Why did I get a son I desperately wanted — but not in the way I got him? Why couldn't I have had my own? I would have loved it then. Everything would have been just as I'd imagined.*
>
> *Life isn't fair, and they've all learnt that now.*
>
> *They all understand the enormity of loss.*

"Damon," Tracy said, holding the book out. "It's all in here from what I saw. This will fill in any missing gaps."

He took it and scanned the pages.

Tracy left him to it, gathering her team — it was pointless searching further when they had what they needed. She sent them home, saying she expected them at work by ten instead of the usual eight, to make up for tonight's overtime.

Once they'd gone, she made sure everything was left tidy, then she had a thought. Did the second Alfie have a wife? Kids?

Sighing, she called in to the station to get the night desk sergeant to run a check. Yes, Alfie had a wife and two kids. Tracy's night wasn't over. She had news of another death to impart, and she wasn't looking forward to it one bit.

CHAPTER TWENTY-SIX

Drained after visiting Mrs Penny Remmings, Tracy shuffled up their garden path after Damon, wanting nothing but a cold glass of wine then bed. Her mind full to bursting, she longed for sleep so she could get some respite before beginning all over again in the morning.

"Shit, I left my phone in the car," she said as Damon opened the door and stepped inside. "Won't be a sec."

"Want me to get it? I don't like you out here by yourself when it's dark." He made to come back out.

"No, no. It's fine. You go on in." She waved him off.

He switched on the hallway light and frowned, then closed the door to.

She dragged her arse to the car, retrieved her phone, and headed back up the garden path. A rustle sounded close, as though someone had kicked through leaves, and she stood stock still, listening for more movement.

Nothing.

Shrugging, she walked on, closer to the side of the house, and an arm shot out and gripped her wrist. Her training kicked in, and she drew the person towards her, swung them round so their back was against her front, and held them tight, both arms around their torso, trapping theirs.

"You don't want to hurt me, do you, Tracy?"

Trepidation settled in Tracy's gut, and the stench of dried blood wafted up.

Oh God, no. Please no . . .

"What. Have. You. Done?" Tracy gritted out quietly in Lisa's ear.

"I had to," Lisa whispered. "She was going to kill me. Did you get my message?"

Tracy thought back to the writing in blood on Ivy's forehead. "I did, but what the fuck do you expect me to *do* about it? The more you hang around here, the more likely you're going to get caught. Damon is just inside. He *knows* it was you tonight and at Costa. How can you have been so stupid as to say your 'gutted' line? The witness bloody *heard* you."

"Oh."

"Yes, oh. So now what? I told you if you came back what I'd do."

"So why don't you then?"

Tracy spun Lisa around and slapped her hard around the face. She stared at her in the light coming through the glass in the top of the front door. "Because I thought you deserved a chance. I thought you'd stop this shit, but you did it again, right on my patch. And you left your *scarf*. What the *hell*?"

"Sorry I didn't have a rainbow one." Lisa smirked.

"Oh. Now that isn't funny. Not funny at all." Images of the rainbow scarf from their childhood flashed in Tracy's mind, the one she'd tied around her head to cover her eyes when John had come to . . . "You're just as sick as them."

"Who?" Lisa canted her head.

"John and *him*, our father."

"We're both sick, you and me, always will be. And that's why you'll let me walk away again." Lisa leant closer. "You can't even take me to the nick for your boyfriend's sake, so what does that say about you?" She strode down the path and, at the bottom, glanced over her shoulder. "See you around, sis."

Then she was gone, as though she'd never been there.

And Tracy was still left with all that deceit.

THE END

THE JOFFE BOOKS STORY

We began in 2014 when Jasper agreed to publish his mum's much-rejected romance novel and it became a bestseller.

Since then we've grown into the largest independent publisher in the UK. We're extremely proud to publish some of the very best writers in the world, including Joy Ellis, Faith Martin, Caro Ramsay, Helen Forrester, Simon Brett and Robert Goddard. Everyone at Joffe Books loves reading and we never forget that it all begins with the magic of an author telling a story.

We are proud to publish talented first-time authors, as well as established writers whose books we love introducing to a new generation of readers.

We won Trade Publisher of the Year at the Independent Publishing Awards in 2023. We have been shortlisted for Independent Publisher of the Year at the British Book Awards for the last four years, and were shortlisted for the Diversity and Inclusivity Award at the 2022 Independent Publishing Awards. In 2023 we were shortlisted for Publisher of the Year at the RNA Industry Awards.

We built this company with your help, and we love to hear from you, so please email us about absolutely anything bookish at: feedback@joffebooks.com.

If you want to receive free books every Friday and hear about all our new releases, join our mailing list: www.joffebooks.com/contact

And when you tell your friends about us, just remember: it's pronounced Joffe as in coffee or toffee!

ALSO BY EMMY ELLIS

DETECTIVE TRACY COLLIER
Book 1: GUTTED
Book 2: CRUSHED

DI BETHANY SMITH
Book 1: THE COLD CALL KILLER
Book 2: THE CREEPY-CRAWLY KILLER
Book 3: THE SCREWDRIVER KILLER
Book 4: THE SCORCHED SKIN KILLER
Book 5: THE STREET PARTY KILLER
Book 6: THE CANDY CANE KILLER
Book 6.5: THE SECRET SANTA KILLER
Book 7: THE MEAT HOOK KILLER
Book 8: THE BLADE KILLER
Book 9: THE SLEDGEHAMMER KILLER

DETECTIVE CAROL WREN MYSTERIES
Book 1: SPITE YOUR FACE
Book 2: HOLD YOUR BREATH
Book 3: GUILT BURNS HOLES
Book 4: BEST SERVED COLD
Book 5: BLOOD RUNS DEEP

Printed in Great Britain
by Amazon

40785695R00118